DENIM DIARIES 4:

BROKEN PROMISES

NOV 09

DENIM DIARIES 4:

BROKEN PROMISES

DARRIEN LEE

www.urbanbooks.com

Urban Books, LLC
1199 Straight Path
West Babylon, NY 11704

Denim Diaries 4: Broken Promises copyright © 2009 Darrien Lee

IISBN-13: 978-1-933967-74-5

ISBN-10: 1-933967-74-9

First Printing December 2009
Printed in the United States of America

10   9   8   7   6   5   4   3   2   1

Distributed by Kensington Publishing Corp.
Submit Wholesale Orders to:
Kensington Publishing Corp.
C/O Penguin Group (USA) Inc.
Attention: Order Processing
405 Murray Hill Parkway
East Rutherford, NJ 07073-2316
Phone: 1-800-526-0275
Fax: 1-800-227-9604

DENIM DIARIES 4:

BROKEN PROMISES

Prologue

The life of a teenager is supposed to be filled with school, fun, love, and friends, not pain, deception, and betrayal. We only get to be teenagers once and to have the most innocent part of us stolen away is not only unforgivable, it's life-changing as well. I pray for myself and my friends each and every day but at this moment I feel like my prayers went unanswered and a beautiful person I know has been damaged forever. I know I'm wrong to blame God, but bad things shouldn't happen to good people so I pray God forgives me on this one. In the meantime I have a friend who needs me to help her fight her battle of redemption. I'm armed with compassion, friendship, and

*love and I have no doubt that we will pre-
vail.
Peace!
D*

Denim wiped away the tears that were stinging
her eyes as she closed her diary and laid across her
bed. She never dreamed she would have to face yet
another devastating event, but it was real and it
had to be dealt with one way or the other. As her
friend, Tiffany Ray, began telling her bits and
pieces about her horrific experience it didn't take
long for Denim's will of compassion to turn to un-
deniable rage. Here is her story.

Tiffany Ray and her BFFs, Anisa and Laurinda,
were inseparable as members of a championship
double Dutch jump rope team known as the Jazzy
Jumpers. On any given afternoon, they could be
found in the driveway of one or the other's house
practicing their routine—after homework, of
course.

It was early fall and school had only been in session for a week. The temperatures were in the mid-
eighties, giving it a summertime feel. As usual the
air conditioners in the classrooms were not working at full capacity. Between the smell of excessive
perfume and body odor, it was hard for Tiffany to

concentrate on what her math teacher was saying. The custodian had brought portable fans into the room but all they did was circulate the funk. A few droplets of sweat appeared on Tiffany's forehead and watching the clock was the only thing that got her through the class period. Once the bell rang, she hurried through the crowd of students making their way to the next class. She was nauseated and making it to the bathroom had become urgent. When she opened the restroom door she thanked God there wasn't a line ahead of her and as she stood in the stall she finally released the tears she'd been holding back all morning. She was concealing a secret and it was one that would shock everyone who knew her.

"Are you okay?" she heard a familiar voice ask from the other side of the door.

Tiffany flushed the toilet and wiped her eyes before exiting the stall.

"I'm fine," she told her friend, Anisa, as she walked over to the sink to wash her hands.

"But I heard you crying," she pointed out as she joined her at the sink. "Are you sure you're okay? Because I know I wasn't hearing things."

"I said I was fine, Anisa," Tiffany snapped as she turned away to wipe some stray tears that had rolled down her cheeks.

"Well, you're not acting fine," Anisa pointed out as she leaned closer to the mirror and reapplied her lip gloss. She watched as Tiffany washed her hands and then splashed cold water on her face.

"You know I'm not going to let you off that easy," Anisa announced as she put the top back on her lip gloss.

"Well, you're wasting your time because I told you I was cool," Tiffany announced.

"Did somebody piss you off?" Anisa asked curiously.

"Listen Anisa, I said I was cool. Don't you know when to mind your business?"

"You are my business. We're best friends, remember? That means we should be able to share everything with each other."

Tiffany could feel the tears beginning to sting her eyes once again so she forced a fake smile and told a huge lie.

"Since you're all up in my Kool-Aid I'll tell you. I started my period. Now are you happy?"

Anisa frowned and asked, "Is that all? Dang, I thought something was wrong."

"You wouldn't listen when I told you I was fine," she repeated, clearly agitated, "but you kept dogging me. You need to learn how to quit nagging people."

Anisa checked her appearance in the mirror once more and said, "I still don't know why you were crying. You knew it was eventually going to happen to you. Tiff, look at it this way, you're a woman now. Congratulations!"

Tiffany rolled her eyes and then pushed past Anisa and quickly exited the restroom. Anisa shook her head and followed her out the door. If she knew the real reason she was crying it would be the top gossip around school but Tiffany would tell no one, not even her best friends.

Chapter One

A few months earlier...

Tiffany's brother, Levar, noticed that the clouds had turned from white to gray and it appeared as though the high humidity was about to give way to some welcome rain. He had hoped that the rain would hold off so he could ride his motorcycle to work but it didn't look like he was going to get that chance. He walked out on the porch and looked up at the dark, swirling clouds. As he stared up at the sky a gust of wind swept over his body and he noticed that a few drops of rain had started falling on the sidewalk.

"What do you mean I can't practice jump rope?" she asked her brother as she burst out the door and joined him on the porch. "Laurinda and Anisa already have plans to come over. You know we practice every evening."

"Not today, so you need to call and cancel,"

Levar replied as he pointed to the raindrops. "It's raining and even if it wasn't, today is my first day at my new job and your sitter starts today."

Tiiffany folded her arms and frowned. She didn't want or need a babysitter but her mother insisted to make sure she was safe in the afternoons until she got home from work. Missing a day of practice was not something Tiffany wanted to do if her crew was going to have any chance of making it to the finals this year. In fact, she was somewhat obsessed when it came to competing but they didn't get nearly fifteen trophies and six first-place ribbons by being lazy.

"Don't you have homework to do anyway?" he asked as he made his way back into the house with his sister close on his heels.

"No, because I did it at school," she answered.

Tiffany followed her brother up the stairs and into his room. She teased her hair as she stared at her reflection in the mirror. She smoothed down her Rihanna T-shirt she'd gotten from a recent concert and then pulled a tube of lip gloss out of her denim shorts pocket. As she gently slid it onto her lips, Levar gave her the protective-brother glare.

"Where did you get that?"

"Momma bought it for me," she proudly admitted.

"I think you're too young for that," he answered.

"All the girls my age wear lip gloss, Levar. Besides, it's rose-colored."

He didn't like her answer because Tiffany already looked older than she was with the curly hairstyle her mother allowed her to wear and the stylish teenage attire. Adding lip gloss to the mix made matters worse. Not to add that her legs were very long and muscular from her years of jumping rope. Levar understood that Tiffany was growing up but in his mind it was too soon and too fast. She was only thirteen years old, but she looked at least sixteen. Her curvaceous body and well-developed chest were causing older boys to stare at her and even approach her on occasion. There were many times he had to shut down their advances and make her actual age known to make them go away. As her brother, it was his responsibility to protect her by any means necessary and he took his job very seriously.

"Tiffany, get out of the mirror and tell me the truth. Do you have homework or not?" he asked as opened his closet. Having stylish athletic gear was his passion and he had approximately fifteen different pair of shoes. He'd worn a pair of his red and white Jordans to school but decided to change into a pair of black Nike Air Force Ones for work.

Tiffany tucked the lip gloss back inside her pocket and then watched her brother change his footwear. She sat down on the bed next to him and smiled.

"Those puppy-dog eyes are not going to work on me today so don't even try it."

"Please, Levar, I might have a few math problems left to do but I'm going to finish them before Momma comes home."

He laughed as he finished putting on his shoes. "I knew you were lying to me. Go do your homework."

"I didn't lie to you, Levar. I really did do most of it at school. I only have about ten problems left to do," Tiffany revealed as she grabbed a pillow off the bed and hugged it.

He stood and put a folder in his book bag.

"I know you, little girl. You can't hide anything from me and you can't do any double Dutch until you handle your business."

"Levar!" she pleaded.

He put his hand playfully over his sister's mouth.

"No, I don't want to hear it. I don't know why you're tripping anyway because it's raining, which means you can't jump rope, so go do your homework."

Tiffany moved her brother's hand and then let

out a loud sigh. She poked her lip out and said, "We could practice in the garage," as she continued to negotiate with her brother. "We'll make it quick, I promise. No more than an hour."

"No," Levar calmly replied without making eye contact with her.

"Please, Levar," she pleaded as she hugged his waist.

He returned a loving hug and then removed her arms.

"I said, no, Tiffany Marie Ray, so drop it."

She put her hands on her hips and stomped the floor with her foot.

"You didn't have to use my whole name," she said, pouting. "Come on, just this once!"

"Have you lost your mind? You know how Momma is about homework. I'm the one who'll get in trouble if she comes home and finds out you didn't get it done."

Contrary to what Levar was saying, he was often guilty of giving in to his sister. She was his heart and he loved her dearly. Tiffany fell back on the bed and put the pillow over her face.

"You know we have another competition coming up in a couple of weeks and if we don't practice we won't have a chance of making it to the finals."

Levar zipped up his book bag and swung it up on his shoulders.

"I know you like to win, sis, but if you bring home one bad grade, Momma's not going to let you go to any more competitions and you know it."

Tiffany stood and said, "Don't make me beg."

He leaned down and kissed her on the cheek and said, "No, now go do your homework."

Tiffany screamed and then loudly stomped off to her room. She had put on one of her best performances to try and get Levar to give in but it didn't work. This new job of his was affecting the hold she had over him. Yes, she was happy he finally got a job but it was putting a strain on her social life already.

Levar was the man of the house since their father, Julius, passed away two years earlier in a car crash. Life for them had been difficult emotionally because their mother, Regina, had been so depressed over her husband's untimely death. He worked nights as an engineering director of a local assembly plant. He was killed after he fell asleep at the wheel and hit a utility pole on his way home from working a double shift. Losing their father dimmed the light in all their hearts but it was their mother who took it the hardest.

Regina and Julius had been high school sweethearts and eighteen years later, when the accident happened, they were still very much in love. The result of losing him caused her to throw herself into nothing but work, church, and her children. She seemed fine with that arrangement but even the children knew she still wasn't happy and needed someone in her life. She had kept most men at bay until a tall, dark, handsome man by the name of Dexter Banks entered her life nearly a year later and immediately swept her off her feet.

Dexter was the owner of Banks Construction Company and when he laid his eyes on Regina it was love at first sight. They met one afternoon while Regina was dining with coworkers at a local restaurant. Dexter and his friend, Paul Lindsey, was sitting across the room when their eyes met. It was an instant attraction and she could hardly stay inside her skin. He was breathtakingly handsome, but for all she knew he was married or gay. But if he was gay, why was he staring at her? Dexter's stares made it hard for her to finish her lunch and it wasn't until he walked over to her table and handed her his business card without speaking so much as a single word that she was finally able to breathe.

Five days passed and Regina still hadn't gotten up the nerve to call the mysterious Dexter Banks. She had to admit that she was intrigued by his ap-

proach but all her pleasant thoughts of him went
out the window when she envisioned him doing
the same move with many other women. It would
be nice to meet someone to share her evenings
with, but getting hooked up with a player was not
on the menu so she threw the card into her trash
can. It wasn't until she grabbed her purse to go
home and noticed the business card in the trash
that she gave him another thought. As she stared at
the card a little voice in her head told her to take a
chance. Regina pulled the card out of the trash
can, studied it for few seconds, and finally got up
enough nerve to dial his number. Overjoyed to
hear her voice, Dexter immediately asked her out
and within a month, they were a hot item.

Regina hadn't dated much since Julius's death
but she did go out on an occasional date. The last
thing she wanted was to act desperate and parade
a group of dysfunctional men in and out of her
children's lives, but there was something different
about Dexter Banks. His charm was so mesmerizing that he became the first man she ever brought
home to meet her children. Their first impression
of him was that he was obviously nice, and seemed
to make their mother very happy. Meeting someone who complemented her life as a mother and

businesswoman was important to her and Dexter seemed to fit just right and now—eight months later—he was her only date.

Levar looked at his watch and knew he had to be leaving for work soon. Since he'd obtained a job, Regina recently hired an eighteen-year-old college student to look after Tiffany for a couple of hours in the afternoon, against Tiffany's wishes, of course. Today she was running late. Levar was starting to get a little nervous. Just as he was about to call the sitter, the telephone rang.

"Hello?"

"Levar, the babysitter can't make it today. She's having car trouble," his mother announced. "Dexter is on his way over to hang out with Tiffany until I get home."

"Why did you call Dexter?" he asked with a frown and a slightly elevated tone of voice.

"Well, son, number one, Dexter has a flexible schedule. Number two, it's your first day at work and you and I both know that you can't be late. Now if you have a better suggestion I'm listening."

Levar thought to himself in silence. The clock was ticking but it seemed like his mother had already made the decision for the both of them whether he approved or not.

"Dexter has never looked after Tiffany alone before," he pointed out.

"Calm down, son," Regina appealed. "I'm sure you've noticed that Tiffany gets along just fine with him."

"I know they do, Momma but—"

She cut him off before he could finish his sentence.

"Levar, I really have to get back to work but if you have a problem with this and want to drive Tiffany all the way over to your grandparents' house, fine, but you're going to be late to work and that's not a good impression to make on your first day."

"Yes, Ma'am," he reluctantly agreed.

Levar knew that everything his mother said was true. Dexter had spent a lot of time with them as a family and sometimes the atmosphere was as if she was already married to him. The only thing missing was the marriage license and an actual ceremony.

"Hold on, Momma," he replied with a slight sigh. "Let me ask Tiffany if she's cool with this because if she's not I'll just have to be late to work."

Regina tapped her ink pen on the desk and held the telephone while Levar called Tiffany into the room.

"What do you want, Levar?" she asked as she

stuffed a handful of popcorn into her mouth. "I'm doing my homework."

"Momma's on the phone. The sitter's having car trouble and won't be able to make it. Dexter is on his way over to hang out until she gets off work. Are you cool with that?"

"I don't know why I need a babysitter anyway. I'm thirteen now! None of my friends have babysitters," she reminded him.

"Tiffany, I don't have time for this. Are you cool with Dexter coming over or not?" he asked anxiously. "If not, I have to take you over to Grand's house."

"Yeah, I'm cool with it," she acknowledged. "I like Dexter. He's fun."

Dexter had won Tiffany's heart right away. He was attentive and he often played board games with her. It also didn't hurt that he was a math genius and was always excited to help her with homework when she didn't understand a math assignment.

"You still have to get your homework done."

She licked her tongue out at him and said, "Give it a rest already. I'll get it done."

Still not convinced it was a good idea to leave Tiffany with Dexter, he asked her once again.

"Are you sure about this, Tiffany?"

"Yes, Levar, I'm sure," she repeated. "Dexter is fun to hang out with."

Levar put the telephone up to his ear and said, "She said it's cool, Momma."

"I knew it would be," she answered as she held up one finger to a coworker who had stuck their head inside her office. "Listen sweetheart, I have to be on a conference call in one minute. Dexter's friend Paul will be with him because they're going to work out when they leave. Before I go, do me a favor and have Dexter shoot me a text when he gets there."

"Okay, Momma. I love you."

She smiled and picked up her laptop and said, "I love you too, son. Have a great day at work."

Levar checked the time on his cell phone and said, "I will."

As soon as he hung up, his cell phone rang again. This time it was his girlfriend, Kyra.

"Hey baby," she greeted him seductively. "Listen, I know you're on your way to work but I wanted to call and wish you good luck on your job."

Levar smiled. Kyra had been his girlfriend for the past five months. She was biracial, the product of a Laotian mother and African American father. Kyra had striking features with dark, mesmerizing eyes, olive skin, and long, wavy auburn hair. She was an all-American point guard on the girls' basketball team thanks to her father, who was a former college standout as a power forward. At nearly five feet nine and thick in all the right places, she already had colleges salivating over her.

"Thanks, Kyra," he replied as he checked his wallet to make sure he had a little cash. "I'm sorry I didn't get a chance to call you earlier. Tiffany's sitter is having car trouble and it's thrown me behind schedule."

"Do you need me to come over?" she asked. "I can be there in about twenty minutes."

"Thanks, but Momma already called Dexter and he should be here any second. I have to get going. Can I call you on my break?"

"Sure, baby. I love you."

"I love you too."

After hanging up the telephone, Levar walked into Tiffany's room and was happy to find her honestly working on her homework but with the music blaring.

He walked across the room and turned down the music.

"How do you expect to get your homework done with Lupe Fiasco bumping so loud?"

"Music helps me concentrate; now turn it back up."

Ignoring her request, he put his hand on her shoulder and said, "I'm leaving as soon as your buddy Dexter gets here. For the last time, are you sure about this? He's bringing his friend Paul with him."

Tiffany sat her pencil down and said, "For the last time, knucklehead, yes! Why are you tripping about it? I didn't see you stressing when you were here all alone playing video games and basketball with him."

"I'm a guy, Tiff."

"And I'm a girl. So what?" she replied.

"You just don't understand, do you?"

Levar was trying his best to make his sister aware of the possible dangers around her. While he had no evidence that Dexter was in any way a threat to his sister, he wasn't ready to completely trust any man around her. Not yet.

"Dexter is almost like having Daddy around again and I like it."

Levar frowned at Tiffany's comment. He wouldn't take it that far but Dexter had been okay to hang out with. Tiffany had taken a liking to him a little more than he had, especially since he'd been so supportive of her with her jump rope competitions and helped her with homework. On occasion, Dexter would go out and give Tiffany and her friends pointers on their routine. Then there was their mom, who had actually found someone who made her laugh again and it was a great sound. She hadn't laughed very much since their father passed away and hearing it again was welcomed.

"By the way, don't even think about trying to con Dexter into letting you practice before you finish your homework."

"Whatever, Levar," she responded as she turned the music back up and turned her attention back to her homework.

Tiffany sometimes hated that Levar knew her so well. She had planned to ask Dexter if her friends could come on over as soon as he left. She could always do her homework later. Now the jig was up.

At that moment, the doorbell rang and Levar hurried back downstairs. When he opened the door, he found Dexter and his friend Paul standing on the porch dressed in sweatsuits and baseball hats. They were holding a couple of bags of what smelled like Chinese food and no telling what else.

Dexter stepped through the door ahead of Paul and patted Levar on the shoulder.

"Hello, Levar. You remember my friend, Paul, don't you?"

Levar closed the door and said, "Yes, hello, Mr. Lindsey."

Paul walked past the young man who was only a couple of inches shorter than him.

"Hello, Levar."

Levar followed Dexter and Paul into the kitchen and watched as they sat the bags on the table.

"How was school today?" Dexter asked as he pulled several glasses from the cabinet.

"It was cool."

"Your mother told me the sitter had car trouble. Today is your first day on your new job, right?"

"Yes, sir."

"Are you excited?" Dexter asked as he pulled two six-packs of Pepsi out of a bag.

"A little bit."

Paul started arranging the boxes of food on the table. He looked over at Levar and asked, "Where do you work?"

"I work at a clinic downtown as a physical therapist intern after school."

"That's great, Levar. It's nice to see young men take an interest in the medical field."

Levar looked at his watch and said, "Thanks, Mr. Lindsey. Hey, Dexter, I really have to get going. Tiffany's in her room doing homework. I'm sure she's going to beg you to let her practice jump rope before she finishes it but don't fall for it."

Dexter smiled and put his hands up in surrender.

He'd seen Tiffany work her charms on Levar and their mother on more than one occasion and he had to admit, she'd gotten to him a couple of times too.

"Don't worry. I'll make sure she finishes her homework. You'd better get going before the rush-hour traffic gets any worse. The rain is definitely going to slow things down more than normal."

Levar slowly backed out of the kitchen as he watched Dexter and Paul arrange the food.

"Okay, I'm out," Levar announced. "Momma wants you to send her a text message to let her know you're here because she's on a conference call."

Dexter clapped his hands together after successfully laying out all the plates, forks, and cups.

"I'll do it right now," he said as he pulled his cell phone out of his jacket pocket. "Before you leave, do me a favor and tell Tiffany to come down so she can eat."

Before Levar could yell for his sister, she burst into the kitchen, rubbing her stomach.

"I smell Chinese food and all I know is there had better be some crab rangoon in one of these boxes."

Dexter chuckled as he pushed a container over to her before continuing to type a text message to Regina.

"I know how much you love them. You know I wouldn't forget them. "

Tiffany opened the container and sniffed the aroma.

"Thank you, Dexter."

"You're welcome. Just save me a couple, if you don't mind."

She nodded in agreement before stuffing a crab rangoon into her mouth.

"Tiffany, aren't you going to say hello to Paul?" Dexter asked.

She smiled over at Paul and said, "Oh yeah, hello, Mr. Lindsey."

"Hello, Tiffany."

"Did you get any egg rolls?" she asked as she opened one of the boxes.

Dexter picked up the receipt and read all the items off to her.

"Let's see, little lady, we have orange chicken, fried rice, crab rangoon, egg rolls, steamed vegetables, and shrimp lo mein."

Paul searched for the box of egg rolls and when he found it he handed it to Tiffany.

"Thank you, Mr. Lindsey."

"How many times do I have to tell you kids it's okay to call me Paul?" he asked.

Levar slowly backed away and said, "Momma never told us we could, Mr. Lindsey."

He smiled and said, "Don't worry, I'll fix that when she gets home."

"Well, it looks like everything's under control here so I'd better get going."

"Good-bye, Levar. Have fun at work and try not to kill anybody," Tiffany she said as a joke.

Dexter and Paul laughed as Dexter picked up his cell phone and read Regina's text message.

"Tiffany, be nice to your brother. It's a big day for him," Dexter reminded her.

Tiffany giggled as she pulled another crab rangoon apart and stuffed it in her mouth.

"He knows I'm just kidding," she replied.

"Drive safely, Levar, and don't worry, I'll make sure Tiffany finishes her homework," Dexter reminded him.

"Thanks," he responded as he put on his jacket. "Tiffany, give me a call if you need me."

"I will," she answered with a smile.

Dexter removed himself from the conversation when his cell phone rang. It was Regina and he spoke softly to her while Tiffany and Paul continued to eat.

"Hey, babe."

"Hello, sweetheart. How's Tiffany?"

He jabbed his fork into the steamed vegetables and said, "Everything here is good. Tiffany's eating dinner and Levar is headed out the door to work."

"Dinner?" she asked as she slid her laptop into the vinyl case. "Did you cook?"

He chuckled.

"No, we stopped at Ling Ling Su's Chinese restaurant on the way over," he revealed. "I'm trying to get Tiffany to save you some but she has a pretty big appetite."

Tiffany rolled her eyes at Dexter's comment. Paul couldn't help but laugh at their interaction. Dexter wasn't lying, though, because he'd been watching her while she ate and it was clear that she had the appetite of most adolescent boys. What worked in her favor was jumping rope, which enabled her to burn the calories off easily.

"Levar, wait!" Tiffany requested as she jumped up from the table when she heard the front door open. She ran out of the kitchen and into the living room and kissed her brother on the cheek.

"Thanks for taking care of me. I know I give you a hard time sometimes but I don't mean to."

He stroked her cheek lovingly and said, "I know, Tiff. We're cool."

That simple gesture from his sister warmed his heart.

Tiffany ran back toward the kitchen, passing Dexter in the hallway. When he got to the front door Levar was putting his duffel bag on the backseat of his Toyota Camry.

As Dexter stood on the porch with the cell phone up to his ear he called out to him.

"Levar, your mother said drive carefully."

"I will," he replied as he pulled away.

Chapter Two

Denim was running a little late to work. She'd spent the last two evenings getting micro-braids and today would be welcoming a new intern into the program at the physical therapy clinic where she worked. The board of education funded a co-op program for high school students who were interested in working in several divisions of the medical field in order to obtain college credits. Physical therapy was one of those fields and she was thankful.

Before pulling out of her driveway she made time to make a few notes in her diary about the events of her day and her sweetheart, Andre Patterson.

Today has been hectic for me. There never seems to be enough hours in the day to get

*what I need done. I love working but it's
taken away so much of my social life. I miss
hanging out with Dré in the afternoons but
hopefully I can cut back on my hours a little
more so we can spend more time together.
Later,
D.*

After closing her diary she backed out of her driveway and proceeded down the street. Dressed in her
Dora the Explorer medical scrubs. She had to con-
stantly change the speed of her wipers to accom-
modate the rain hitting her windshield. One minute
the rain was falling in a steady drizzle, the next
minute it was raining cats and dogs. This made her
extra happy that she'd gotten her braids because
they were low maintenance.

When the next traffic light turned red, she looked
at the time. She hated being late to work. Number
one, it didn't set a good example to the new intern
and secondly, it was just not something she liked
to do. As she sat there waiting for the green light
her cell phone rang. She looked at the caller ID and
saw Drés' name pop up.

"Hello, baby. I can only take a second because
the light is red. What's up?"

"That's cool. Are you on your way to the clinic?"

"Yeah and it's raining like crazy out here. What are you doing?"

"Besides thinking about you," he admitted, "I'm getting ready to go over to the school to work on the mural."

Dré was not only an outstanding basketball athlete, he was also a talented artist and the board of education had commissioned him to paint an educational mural on the wall of the main entrance of his high school, Langley High.

"I can't wait to see the finished product. I know it's going to be beautiful."

"Thanks. They said they might get me to do some of the other schools too."

"So, Prime Time, what are you going to do with all that money they're paying you?" she asked.

Prime Time was his screen name on his e-mail address and she used it often in conversations with him.

"A little bit of this and a little bit of that," he joked. "Seriously, I haven't given it a lot of thought. I know most of it is going into my savings."

"Sounds like a plan to me and even though I'm one of your biggest fans, you're worth every penny and then some."

He blushed and said, "Thanks, babe."

The traffic light turned green and Denim proceeded through the light.

"Well, the light's green so I'd better get off this phone since it's raining. I'll call you later."

"Okay and be careful. I love you."

"I love you to, Dré."

Denim quickly hung up the telephone and fifteen minutes later she pulled into the parking lot of the physical therapy clinic where she worked after school three days a week and one Saturday a month. She quickly found a parking spot, locked her car, and hurried inside the building.

Levar listened attentively to the physical therapist as he went over the day's schedule. It was the first day he would have the honor of working with Denim. He was excited to be working in her company because when she walked in he remembered she was just as beautiful as the first day they met.

"Good morning, everybody," Denim greeted the staff as she entered the office and put her wet umbrella in a plastic bag. "It's nasty out there."

Levar smiled.

The physical therapist in charge of interns, Tony Vega, looked at his watch and said, "You cut it pretty close today, Denim."

She giggled and she pulled her braids up into a ponytail.

"Your watch is at least ten minutes fast, Tony, and you know it so don't even try that on me today."

Tony Vega was in his early forties and had been a physical therapist for over fifteen years.

She sniffed in the air and asked, "Is that dough-nuts and coffee that I smell?"

Tony chuckled.

"Of course. You know we always have coffee, juice, and pastries for the patients every Wednes-day, not that they ever get any because of you."

She put her hands on her hips and said, "Now you know you're lying."

With a grin on his face, Tony waved her over and said, "Yes, I was just teasing you. Now let's get down to business. You remember our new intern, Levar Ray, right?"

"Yes, hello, Levar," she greeted him with a smile.

"Hello, Denim," Levar replied shyly. "It's nice seeing you again."

"I want you two to work together as a team today and Denim, I want you to take Levar step-by-step through the afternoon."

She saluted Tony and jokingly said, "Will do, boss."

Tony shook his head and said, "Get to work, guys, and if you need me, just holler."

Denim took Levar behind the counter and showed him how to log into patient information. As she typed on the computer she asked, "So how has it been so far?"

"It's been cool," Levar replied. "I'm glad I finished my orientation class today. I'm ready to get to work."

"Good for you. Have I missed anything so far?" she asked as she glanced up at him.

He took a whiff of her perfume and softly said, "No, but there's some interesting patients who come here. I'll be happier once I get used to the routine and everyone."

Levar could barely make eye contact with Denim but something told her that it was nervousness more so than shyness. She wanted him to be comfortable working with her so she did her best to come up with ways to ease his nerves.

"Levar, are you shy or are you still a little nervous about the job?" she asked curiously.

He blushed and said, "I'm just trying to absorb everything you're showing me."

She'd made quite an impression on him already and being in close proximity made it hard for him to concentrate.

"You'll be fine. It takes time and I have no doubt that you're on the right track."

"Thanks."

Denim leaned in close and whispered to him. "Want to know a secret?"

"Sure," he answered.

"Tony tries to act like a drill sergeant but he's really a teddy bear so don't let him mess with your head."

Tony noticed Denim whispering to Levar and pointing in his direction. He figured she was telling him some type of story about him so he said, "Don't believe anything she's telling you."

Denim and Levar looked at each other and laughed together.

Tony walked over to the two and said, "Levar, you've done a great job today and I'll do my best to give you the best training possible. I'm saying this because I want all my interns to not only love their jobs but love the profession as well."

"I'd like that as well, sir," Levar responded.

"No *sirs* around here. We work on first-name basis except when it comes to our patients. Then by all means, use *sir* and *ma'am*."

"I can do that, Tony," Levar replied as he glanced over at Denim, who was now talking to the office secretary. He was mesmerized as he watched her twirl one of her braids around her finger and giggle at something the secretary said to her. She was not only beautiful but she was nice too. He could see himself falling for her but he already had a girlfriend and he had to make sure he remembered that.

Denim turned toward Levar and caught him staring at her. She walked over to him and put her hand on his shoulder.

"Well, Levar, are you ready to show me what you got?"

"I'm as ready as I'm going to be. I just hope you can handle my moves," Levar joked and he did a little dance step.

Denim giggled.

Tony interrupted the pair and alerted them to the fact that another patient had arrived.

"Come on, Levar. Let's get to work."

An hour later, Levar said, "Wow, this is a lot to take in. I just hope I don't mess up."

"Don't stress over it, Levar, because you *will* mess up. We all have. Besides, it's no big deal unless you kill somebody."

Levar froze in his tracks.

Denim turned to him and noticed that he looked like a deer caught in the headlights. She burst out laughing.

"I was just kidding, Levar. Don't freak out on me."

"I'm not. It's just funny because my sister said the same thing to me."

"How old is your sister?" Denim asked.

"She's thirteen, but she looks like she's sixteen."

Denim smiled. "You guys are close, huh?"

Levar blushed and said, "Very. She's my heart."

"That's sweet. Me and my brother have a similar relationship."

"Really? Is he younger or older than you?"

"He's twenty-one years old and in college in Atlanta. He's my best friend."

"Cool."

Denim went on to show Levar how to work the whirlpool and how to monitor patients while they were in the spa.

"I'll have this down in little or no time. You're a great teacher."

Denim locked eyes with her new coworker. His comment was somewhat flirty and she realized she might have to keep her guard up around Levar Ray. He was almost as cute as Dré and compromising her relationship was the last thing she would ever do.

Regina put the last folder in the file cabinet and closed the drawer. She glanced over at the family portrait on her desk taken years earlier. She looked at her husband's eyes and smiled. They were so full of life and love and she missed him terribly. Thankfully, Dexter had come into her life just when all hope of ever loving again seemed lost. The children and their well-being was important to her but Dexter was a breath of fresh air and her love for him was growing stronger every minute of each day. She ran her hands through her hair before turning off her laptop. It had been a long day and she was anxious to get home.

The rain had finally stopped and it was still very humid, but that didn't stop Tiffany and her friends from getting in an hour of practice after she finished her homework. Paul was called into work so he had to cancel his work-out session with Dexter. To pass the time he decided to go outside and help Tiffany and her friends with their routine.

"Okay, girls, remember, you have to make sure you keep the beat in your head as you're jumping," Dexter explained to Tiffany, Anisa, and Laurinda.

"We already have the beat in our head, Dexter," Tiffany replied. "What we need help with is coming up with some new moves."

He folded his arms and asked, "When is the competition?"

"It's a month from Saturday and we're not even close to being ready for it," Anisa answered.

"Don't worry about that. You'll be ready. That means you only have about two weeks to come up with some new moves. The other two weeks, just concentrate on making the routine perfect."

Tiffany, Anisa, and Laurinda nodded in agreement.

"There's a lot of good teams out there," Anisa pointed out. "We need something fresh and hot."

He thought for a minute and then said, "I have an idea. You'll have your new moves but you're going to have to get your parents' permission first."

Tiffany twirled the jump rope over her head like a lasso and asked, "What's this big idea, Dexter?"

"Have you guys seen any of the movies about clown dancing or krumping?"

"I have," Laurinda replied. "But what does that have to do with coming up with new moves?"

"Oh, I get it," Anisa answered with a huge smile on her face. "We could probably put some of the krumping moves in our routine."

"How is that possible?" Tiffany asked. "We can't turn the ropes, jump, and do all those wild body moves that krumpers do."

"Yes you can if you make it your own," Dexter

suggested. "All you have to do is take the krumping and tone it down a little to make it work with the jump rope."

The three girls looked at each other in silence.

"It won't hurt to try it," Laurinda added.

"Look, I happen to know a couple of kids who are very good at it but they live in Chesterfield. Their dad works for me. If it's okay with your parents I could take you guys over to the park where they hang out so you can see them in action."

Anisa sighed with disappointment.

"I don't think my parents will let me go all the way up to Chesterfield, Mr. Banks."

He smiled.

"I understand, Anisa. Why don't you ask them to come with us? If they're going to support you and your team they need to be involved in the training too."

"It's not that easy, Mr. Banks. My mom works two jobs."

Laurinda sat down in the driveway and said, "My mom would probably like to go but she's been yelling about gas prices so I don't know if she'll want to drive all the way to Chesterfield."

"How many people can fit into your SUV, Dexter?" Tiffany asked as she pointed at his vehicle.

He looked over at his black Infiniti QX56 and said, "It seats seven. That will seat you three, Laurinda's mom, and Regina. Anisa, since your mom is working two jobs and can't go, have her call Tiffany's mom so she can talk to her about our field trip. Deal?"

The three girls screamed and hugged each other and then smacked high fives all around, Dexter included.

"Great!" Dexter yelled, then looked at his watch and said, "okay, ladies, it's getting late and you have school tomorrow. Get your things so Tiffany and I can drive you home."

"It's okay, Mr. Banks, we can walk," Anisa replied.

He pulled his keys out of his pocket and said, "No you're not. I wouldn't feel right letting you girls walk home by yourselves."

Laurinda giggled and said, "We just live two streets over."

With a serious expression on his face, he put his hand on their shoulders and said, "I know, but a lot of kids have disappeared out of their own yards. I'm not about to take a chance with you guys."

"Okay, Mr. Banks," Laurinda replied before handing Tiffany the jump ropes so she could put them away in the garage. They climbed into the truck and just as they were about to leave, Regina pulled in beside them and rolled down the window.

"Where are you guys headed?" she asked with a loving smile on her face.

"I'm taking Laurinda and Anisa home. They've been practicing their routine for the competition and I didn't want them walking home by themselves."

Regina climbed out of her car and made her way over to the driver's-side window. She leaned in and gave Dexter a sensual kiss on the lips.

Tiffany rolled her eyes with embarrassment while Anisa and Laurinda giggled from the backseat.

"That's sweet of you, but I could drive them if you want me to."

"No, I got it."

Seeing Dexter with the girls warmed Regina's heart. He never had children but you wouldn't know by the patience, love, and attentiveness he had with her children. She was sure in her heart, mind, and soul that Dexter was God sent and that her prayers had been answered.

"Are you sure?" she asked again, making sure he didn't feel obligated to drive the girls home.

"Of course I'm sure," he replied as he caressed her hand. "We had a great practice today."

"We?" Regina asked curiously.

"Yes, Mrs. Regina, Mr. Banks helped us practice today," Laurinda revealed.

"Well, that is nice of Mr. Banks. How are you girls doing?" she asked as she waved at Anisa and Laurinda.

"Hi Ms. Regina," they replied in unison.

"Do you want to ride with us, Momma?" Tiffany asked.

"No, you guys go ahead. I'm starving and I want to get out of these heels and this suit."

Dexter put the truck in reverse and whispered, "If you wait fifteen minutes or so I can give you a little help with that and then some."

"You're so naughty," she replied as she playfully spanked his hand. "Drive safely and hurry back. I hope you guys saved me some dinner."

"Don't worry, we did. See you in a few."

Regina stepped away from the vehicle and waved good-bye to Dexter and the girls.

Chapter Three

It was nearly nine o'clock as Tiffany laid across her bed talking to Anisa and Laurinda on a three-way call.

"I just finished watching that documentary called *Rize* and now I see what Dexter was talking about. When they showed some of the moves in slow motion, I could see us doing some of them," she explained. "All we have to do is slow down the moves."

Anisa yawned.

"Sounds like a plan. Look, I'm getting sleepy. I'll see you guys tomorrow."

"Me too," Laurinda added.

"Okay, I need to get off the phone anyway. Levar should be home soon and I want to find out what he did at work today. Good night, Jazzy Jumpers."

In union, Anisa and Laurinda answered, "Good night."

Tiffany hung up the telephone and rolled over onto her stomach. As she laid there she admired all the trophies and ribbons they'd won from their jump rope competitions. She couldn't help but smile with satisfaction and couldn't wait to add the regional championship trophy to their collection.

"What are you thinking about?" Levar asked as he surprised his sister.

She jumped off the bed and ran over and hugged his neck as he stood in the doorway.

"Levar! When did you get home?"

He smiled and gave her a kiss on the cheek.

"I just got here. I thought you would be asleep by the time I got home. At least you have on your pajamas."

She looked down at her Elmo pajamas before she sat on the side of her bed.

"No way. I wanted to wait up for you."

He walked farther into her room and pushed all her stuffed animals out of her chair before sitting down.

"How did everything go today with Dexter and his friend Paul?" he asked.

"We had a good time—well, Mr. Lindsey had to leave but after I finished my homework, Dexter coached me and my crew on our new jump rope routine."

Levar picked up a stuffed frog and stared at his sister.

"You did finish, didn't you?"

"Yes, big brother, and for your information Dexter helped me."

He smiled with satisfaction.

"Good. Now what does Dexter know about jumping rope?"

She shrugged her shoulders and said, "I don't know, but he had a lot of good ideas."

With a smirk on his face, he asked, "Like what?"

Tiffany walked over and took the frog out of her brother's hand.

"If you must know, he suggested that we put some krumping moves in our routine."

"Krumping?" he asked. "How are y'all going to krump and jump rope at the same time?"

"I don't know, but it's worth trying."

"That's stupid, Tiffany," he answered as he tried to grab the frog out of her hands but she held it away from him.

"Not really. I watched that movie *Rize* tonight and I can kind of see what he was talking about."

"Whatever. I still didn't like you being here alone with Dexter."

Tiffany studied her brother's expression as she sat back down on the bed.

"Why don't you like Dexter?"

"It's not that I don't like him, Tiff. I just don't know him very well, which means I don't trust him."

She looked at her brother, who seemed to stare across the room in a daze as he spoke.

"He's not Daddy, big brother."

Levar looked at his sister with a frown on his face. "I don't need you to tell me that."

Tiffany walked over to Levar and sat on the ottoman in front of the chair. She finally handed him the stuffed green frog and said, "Momma really likes Dexter. Don't you see how her face lights up when he's around?"

He tugged on her ear playfully and said, "Yeah, I noticed. I just don't want her to get hurt."

"He's really cool, Levar. Just give him a chance, for Momma's sake."

Levar smiled and tousled her hair before standing.

"I'll think about it. Now give me a hug."

Tiffany jumped in her brother's arms and said, "I love you, Levar. Good night."

He tossed her onto her bed playfully and said, "I love you too. Good night, sis."

She giggled and turned off the lamp on the night-stand and closed her eyes.

Levar made his way down the hallway to his room. Just as he was about to enter, Regina came up the stairs and met him in the hallway.

"Is your sister asleep?"

"Not yet, but she's on her way."

Regina folded her arms and leaned against the wall. "So how was your first day on the job?"

"It was good. I really like physical therapy. I can see myself doing it for a living."

She cupped her son's face and smiled. He was so much like his father, physically and emotionally and she loved him dearly.

She released him and said, "I'm glad. I knew you had it in you. You have a nurturing spirit just like your father."

Levar blushed and said, "Thanks."

There was an awkward silence between them for a moment. It was as if they were waiting on the other to reveal or ask something important but they were afraid to.

"Is Dexter still here?" Levar asked sarcastically.

"No, baby, he's gone. Why?" she asked curiously.

Levar lowered his head and mumbled, "No reason. I was just wondering."

Regina linked her arm with son's arm and walked him into his room.

She patted the edge of his bed with her hand and said, "Sit down, son, I want to talk to you for a second."

Levar sat his book bag down on the floor and powered up his laptop before sitting. Without making eye contact with her he asked, "What do you want to talk about?"

"Dexter."

"Come on, Mom," he replied as he tried to get up.

She grabbed his wrist, stopping him, and said, "No, I want to know what the problem is with you and Dexter. As far as I know he hasn't given you any reason not to like him. Talk to me, son."

"I don't know, Mom, I just don't trust him, especially around Tiffany. He's always smiling and hugging on her like he's known us for years," he revealed. "Personally, I wish he'd keep his damn hands to himself."

She folded her arms and angrily said, "I don't want you using that kind of language, especially with me."

"I'm sorry."

"Levar, you don't trust any male around Tiffany and I love that about you, but Dexter would never hurt Tiffany. He hugs her because he loves her and if you would give him a chance, he'd hug you too."

He laid back on his bed and said, "I'll pass on that one, Momma, but why do you think he can be trusted. What do you really know about him?"

Regina took Levar's hands into hers and said, "I know he cares about me, you, and your sister. I know he's a hardworking man who lost someone he loved just like we did. He doesn't have children and that's something he said he's always wanted. He's crazy about you guys and you'll see it if you just give him a chance."

Levar gave his mother's hands a gentle squeeze and said, "I don't want to see you get hurt again."

She hugged his neck and said, "I love you for wanting to protect my heart but you have to trust me and let me do this on my own. That would the best birthday present you could ever give me."

"Mom . . ."

"Levar, work with me on this. I'm happy. Okay?"

He forced a smile and said, "I'll try."

"Good," she replied, after which she kissed his cheek and stood.

"Sweet dreams, son."

"Good night, Momma."

As she walked toward the door she said, "I want to hear more about your job in the morning."

"Okay."

She closed the door, leaving Levar to his thoughts. He decided he would lighten up a little bit but he would definitely keep an eye on Dexter.

Down the hallway Regina prepared for bed. She pulled back the lavender and white comforter on her king-sized bed. She had hoped that Dexter would've stayed over tonight but he reminded her that he had to be at his work site before dawn the next morning. She had become accustomed to his early mornings and late nights. That was the life of a business owner, especially one in the construction business.

Dexter arrived at work before most people thought about getting out of bed. He was very dedicated and involved with his company. That's why he was more than just the owner. He was definitely a hands-on owner. He could often be found working alongside his men in a hard hat and work boots. Then when he needed to rock a designer business suit for his high-powered meetings he was able to do that with intelligence and class as well. The only thing missing in his life now was the family he longed for. He'd lost his girlfriend suddenly four years earlier to a brain aneurysm days before he had planned to propose to her. He hadn't dated seriously since he met Regina.

Dexter entered his small trailer office, took off his hard hat, and laid it on his desk. His latest building project was going great and he was two months ahead of the original completion date. As he sat at his desk, he glanced down at several rolls of blueprints. After opening one of the blueprints, his mind wandered to Regina and how much she meant to him. She was more than a woman, she was a mother, friend, and lover and if he had things his way, he'd make her his wife. As he continued to daydream he thought about Levar and Tiffany, two wonderful but heartbroken children who were still hurting from the tragic loss of their father. He knew he would have to continue to be compassionate to their feelings and let them know he wasn't trying to replace their father, just be the best stepfather he could be and love them and their mother. Tiffany seemed to be coming along just fine even though she was a serious daddy's girl. Levar was another story. After his father's death he became the man of the house and for understandable reasons, he seemed to carry a deep resentment that he was dating Regina. It was going to be harder to get Levar to come around but in time, Dexter hope he would be accepted into the family.

"Mr. Banks, you're needed on the third floor," the voice said over the two-way radio.

He picked up his radio and stood.

"I'll be right there. Breakfast is in thirty minutes. Make sure the crew finishes up whatever they're working on before stopping to eat."

"Will do, boss," the voice replied over the radio.

Dexter had often provided breakfast for his men since they had to come in so early. It was the least he could do since many of them had families and worked long hours just like he did. He grabbed his hard hat and headed over to the third floor of the building.

Levar couldn't sleep. No matter what he did, he just couldn't fall asleep. As he laid there staring at the ceiling he thought about the conversation he'd had with his mother. She seemed so sure about Dexter but he wasn't and he never would be until he knew his intentions. Angry, he threw back the comforter and sat on the side of the bed. The clock said four AM, which left only about two hours until he would have to be up for school. He had a long day ahead of him but it didn't seem like sleep was on the menu. He had too much on his mind.

Down the hallway, Tiffany tossed and turned in her sleep. She was anxious to get started on their new routine for the regional double Dutch competition. It was going to be the biggest in the region and if they won it would send them to nationals once and for all. Over the past few years they had come up short at regionals, each time edged out by older and better teams. Winning would open a lot of doors for them and also help pay for college. She just wished her father could have lived to witness her recent accomplishments and the ones yet to come.

Across town, Denim giggled quietly so she wouldn't wake up her parents. She had spent yet another night talking all night on the telephone with Dré.

"I bet Levar looks like a pencil with big ears."

"He does not." Denim defended her new coworker.

"So you think he's cute?"

She hugged her pillow and said, "As a matter of fact, I do. He's sweet too."

"Maybe I need to come by there and let him know you're my girl."

"Dré, you're so silly. Every guy doesn't want to hook up with me."

"Then they must be gay because a guy would have to be blind not to want to hook up with you," he joked.

"He's not gay," she replied before yawning. "He's as much man as you are, silly."

Dré smiled and asked, "Is that right?"

"Yes."

"And how would you know that, Miss Mitchell?"

"Let's just say I have a sixth sense on the subject."

"If you say so, babe. I guess we need to turn in for a couple of hours."

Denim looked at her clock and yawned once more.

"Yeah, I am getting a little sleepy."

"If you let me come over I'll make sure you go right to sleep," Dré suggested seductively.

"Go take a cold shower, Prime Time. That's all you think about."

"Like you don't," he quickly replied. "And to be honest, you're all I think about. I can't help it that I have the hottest girl in school."

"Ahhh, you're so sweet and I love you."

"I love you too. Now, go to bed. I'll see you in a couple of hours."

"Good night, baby."

"Don't you mean good morning?"

The young lovers hung up the telephone and finally turned in for what was left of the morning.

* * *

The next afternoon, Tiffany scooped a forkful of lasagna as she sat in the school cafeteria with her friends.

"We're going to win this time. I could barely sleep last night thinking about it."

Laurinda picked up her spoon and took a bite of her fruit cocktail and with frustration in her voice said, "We'd better, because I'm sick of losing."

"We lost in the regional tournament, not the pre-liminaries," Tiffany reminded her teammates. "And we won all the local contests."

"I'm sick of losing too," Anisa replied with a sigh.

Tiffany slammed her fork down on her tray and stared at her two friends.

"What is wrong with you guys? You act like we haven't won any trophies or ribbons. I don't need all this negativity."

"Excuse me!" Laurinda yelled and then giggled.

Students sitting nearby turned and stared at the trio.

Tiffany stared back at the students and then rolled her eyes. "Listen, you eggheads. We all work hard to win but if you guys are not up for it, let me know and I'll get a new team. I'm not going to stop until we win the nationals. So what's it going to be?"

Anisa and Laurinda looked at each other in silence for a few seconds. They knew they had touched a nerve with Tiffany and she could be quiet passionate about jumping rope. She wasn't one to give up easy and didn't want them to be either

"Okay, Tiffany, calm down. You don't have to get all crazy on us," Anisa stated before taking a sip of fruit punch.

"You two make me crazy," Tiffany replied and she ran her fingers through her curly hair.

"I'm just saying," Anisa answered back. "Look, Tiffany, we want to win but you're starting to get a little obsessed."

"Obsessed?" Tiffany responded. "I'm obsessed? Let me tell you why this should mean as much to you as it does me. I don't know about you, but I could use the scholarship money and the last time I checked none of your parents were rich either."

"You don't have to be rich to go to college," Laurinda added. "You can get student loans and financial aid."

"Why go through all that if you don't have to?" Tiffany asked. "All I'm saying is since my dad died, things have been okay for us but I know it's going to be hard for my mom to send Levar to college, let alone me too. I just want to do something to help my mom."

"Please!" Anisa replied as she rolled her eyes. "Your mom is dating Mr. Banks and he's rich."

"My mom is dating him, fool! While Dexter does take us out to dinner and stuff like that he doesn't have to spend a dime on us. We're not his kids!"

"I know you're not his kids but—"

"But nothing, Anisa!" Tiffany yelled as tears ran down her face. "After my dad died, my mom did what she had to do. Not that it's any of your business, but she paid off the house, cars, and other bills with the insurance money so we wouldn't have to move. There's no money left over for college."

Anisa now felt bad that she'd even brought up the subject since it was obvious that the loss of Tiffany's father was still a sensitive subject. She'd unintentionally hurt her best friend's feelings and made her cry. Lauinda reached across the table and held Tiffany's hand to comfort her.

"Don't cry, Tiffany. I know you miss your dad but I see how Mr. Banks looks at your mom. If you ask me, I don't think you and your family have a thing to worry about as far as money is concerned. "

Tiffany pulled her hand away and wiped a couple of tears off her cheeks.

"I don't care about Dexter's money. While he's cool and all, I would give anything to have my dad back."

Tears were now filling Anisa's eyes.

"I'm sorry, Tiffany. I didn't mean to make you sad about your dad. Listen, count me in. I'm willing to practice harder so we can win the nationals. What about you, Laurinda?"

Laurinda held her fist out and said, "I'm in."

All three girls bumped their fists together and with smiles, picked up their moods and finished their lunch before returning to class.

Levar opened his locker and pulled out his geometry book. When he turned around, Kyra was standing there with her arms folded.

"Hey stranger," she called out to him.

He walked over to her and gave her a kiss on her lips.

"Hey yourself. What's up?"

She put her hands on her hips in disgust.

"You tell me. I never see you anymore."

Levar lowered his head and softly replied, "I know and I'm sorry. You know I'm working now so I don't have a lot of free time."

"And? You have a cell phone and e-mail. Can't a girl get a text, a phone call or something?"

"You're right," he said as he softly touched her cheek. "I'll do better."

A slight smile appeared on Kyra's face as she easily forgave him.

"Apology accepted." She put her arm around his waist and announced, "You have a lot of making up to do with me."

He hugged her lovingly and said, "I think I can arrange that."

She released him and asked, "So how is this new job of yours?"

"It's good. I like it. The people there are cool and I'm learning a lot."

The young couple walked down the hallway together. Kyra smiled and slid her arm around his waist and said, "Maybe you can get me some physical therapy."

"I think I can arrange that," he answered with a huge smile on his face. "You know I have magic hands."

Kyra giggled.

"Don't forget my mom's birthday party is this weekend," he reminded her. "She's so excited and been reminding me of it nearly every day."

"I wouldn't miss it for the world," she replied as she walked with Levar to their next class.

Chapter Four

Tiffany and her crew had gotten a lot of help and ideas from the krumpers, now all they had to do was put their ideas into a routine. As she sat on the side of the bed lacing up her lime-green Nike, she sent Anisa and Laurinda dual text messages.

Seconds later there was a soft knock on the door. When she answered it, she found Levar standing on the outside.

"What are you doing up so early? It's Saturday."

She smiled and said, "I have jump rope practice. Why are you up?"

He walked into her room and sat down in a nearby chair.

"I guess because I heard you moving around in here."

"I'm sorry, Levar. I was trying to be quiet."

He waved her off and said, "It's not your fault. Where are you practicing at?"

"We were going to meet in the park down the street."

Levar frowned.

"Tiffany, it's seven o'clock in the morning. You, Anisa, and Laurinda are not going to any park at seven AM all alone. Give them a call them and let them know I'll pick them up with their parents' permission and stay with you guys until you finish practicing."

"Really?"

"You're not practicing otherwise unless you come here and that's out of the question since it's so early. You'll wake up the neighborhood with all that noise. Give me twenty minutes to shower and get dressed and I'll meet you downstairs."

"Thank you, Levar," she replied as she hurriedly sent updated text messages to both of her friends.

Levar hadn't been able to spend much time with his sister or Kyra lately because of his job. Today he'd hoped to make up for lost time with both of them because they were two of the most important women in his life. His family came first but Kyra was an angel and had stayed by his side during his darkest hour. She had been God sent after losing his father and her presence helped him get through the most painful experience in his life.

As he climbed inside his car next to Tiffany and turned the ignition, he called Kyra.

"Hello?" her sleepy voice answered.

"Hey babe, get up. I want to take you to breakfast."

Kyra turned over and looked at the clock and then closed her eyes again.

"Do you know what time it is?" she asked, still somewhat delirious.

"Of course I do," he replied. "Now get up and put some clothes on. I have to take Tiffany and her crew to the park for practice and I want you to go with me."

She finally sat up and let out a big yawn.

"I thought you said you were taking me to breakfast."

"I am, after Tiffany and her entourage finishes practice. So are you going to come or not?"

Kyra threw back her comforter and smiled.

"You'd better be glad I love you. I wouldn't get up early for just anyone. I'll be ready by the time you get here."

"Cool," Levar replied before hanging up.

Tiffany looked over at him and asked, "Why do you have that goofy look on your face?"

He drove down the street toward Laurinda's house and glanced in the rearview mirror.

"I don't have a goofy look on my face. You're tripping."

Tiffany giggled.

"I'm just messing with you. I know you like Kyra."

He hit her playfully on the leg and said, "She's sweet like you. That's why I'm dating her."

"Ahh," Tiffany responded as she put her hand over her heart.

Levar pulled up in front of Laurinda's house and walked to the door to greet her father. As they walked off he said, "Don't worry, sir. I'll watch them like a hawk."

"Drive safely, Levar."

He opened the car for Laurinda and said, "I will."

Next stop was to Anisa's house. When they pulled up, she was already on the porch waiting for them. Levar still exited the vehicle and met Anisa's mother at the door.

"Hello, Levar. It's nice of you to take the girls to practice."

"It's okay, Mrs. Parker. I support them with anything that keeps them off the streets and out of trouble."

"Amen to that," she answered as she waved to

him as he made his way back to the car. After driving off, his last stop was at Kyra's house. It seemed like he jumped out of the car before he put it in park.

"Dang, Levar," Tiffany teased as she climbed out of the front seat and into the backseat with her friends. "Slow down, Levar, you don't have to run. Kyra's not going anywhere."

Tiffany's comment made Anisa and Laurinda giggle. While Levar was away Laurinda asked, "Tiffany, do you think Levar and Kyra have. . . . you know."

"What, Laurinda? Had sex?" Anisa yelled.

"Shhh, you two," Tiffany hushed them.

"Well? Do you?" Laurinda asked again.

"I don't know. Levar doesn't talk to me about his love life."

"She is pretty and she has a body out of this world," Anisa pointed out. "He's a boy and that's all boys think about."

"Not all boys, Anisa. Dang! Sounds like that's all you think about," Tiffany replied with frustration. "Since we're talking about it, have you?"

She smiled and said, "Once."

"You're lying!" Laurinda yelled.

"No I'm not!" Anisa defended herself.

Tiffany looked at Anisa with curiosity and asked,

"Why would you do something like that with some-one you don't love? You're stupid."

"I'm not stupid and what makes you think I'm not in love?" Anisa asked Tiffany, who ignored her.

"Who was it?" Laurinda asked. It was obvious that she was more interested in the subject than Tiffany was.

"I don't kiss and tell, but I will tell you that he's in the tenth grade and fine as hell."

"You're nasty," Laurinda added. "He's going to dog you."

Anisa poked Laurinda in the forehead and said, "Don't hate."

"Be quiet, here comes Levar and Kyra," Tiffany announced.

The three girls sat in the backseat quietly as Kyra and Levar climbed into the car.

"Good morning, ladies," Kyra greeted them.

"Good morning," the three girls replied in uni-son.

"Tiffany, I haven't seen you in a while, what's up beside the competition."

"Nothing," she answered solemnly as Levar backed out of Kyra's driveway.

Kyra pulled down the sun visor so she could study Tiffany's expression in the mirror.

"What's wrong with Tiffany?" she asked Levar as she applied lip gloss to her soft lips.

He turned up the radio and said, "She's cool, just anxious to practice. They really want to win this year."

"Well, they're really good. I hope they win too," she said before pushing the sun visor back into place. "I'm starving. Where are we going for breakfast?"

"I thought we'd go to IHOP. Their pancakes are da bomb."

She glanced over her shoulder and asked, "Are they going to breakfast too?"

"Nah, just Tiffany, if that's cool with you."

Kyra smiled and said, "You know I love Tiffany. I only asked because I wasn't sure if you could afford to buy everyone's breakfast."

"I could, but I'm not going to this time. Now if they win the competition, dinner's on me."

She leaned over and kissed him on the cheek as he pulled into the park's entrance.

"I like the sound of that. You're so sweet and generous."

"It's no big deal. I just like taking care of the people I love."

Kyra smiled and caressed his arm.

"We're here, ladies, so let's get this practice started because I have a date with my baby."

Tiffany and her friends filed out of the backseat and then pulled their jump ropes out of the trunk. Laurinda handed Levar a CD to put in the car's stereo as they warmed up with a series of jumps and stretches on the empty basketball court.

Kyra sat on the hood of his car and tugged at the strings on her pink Ecko hoodie.

"I don't see how they do it. My legs are too long and would just get in the way. It's a wonder I can find jeans to fit me."

Levar ran his hands down her long, shapely legs and said, "Your legs are perfect in every way and I love the way your jeans fit your body."

She blushed and said, "Levar, not in front of the children."

He ignored what Kyra said and then pulled her into his arms for a long-awaited kiss. Tiffany and her friends noticed the young couple. Anisa and Laurinda blushed while Tiffany said, "Why are you guys acting so silly? I've seen Levar and Kyra kiss a thousand times and Anisa, I know you're not blushing after your public service announcement."

"I think she lied," Laurinda announced. "If she was all that experienced, kissing wouldn't make her blush."

Anisa pointed her finger in Laurinda's face and

said, "Think what you want. I don't have to prove anything to you."

"You're the one who was bragging earlier, not me," Laurinda responded as she twirled the rope.

"Look! We're not here to argue or talk about Anisa's so-called love life. Can we please practice? Levar is not going to hang around here forever," Tiffany revealed.

"I'm ready," Laurinda replied.

"I'm ready too," Anisa followed up.

"Good, now let's do this," Tiffany urged her teammates right before they started their routine.

Denim had decided that she was going to start jogging to stay in shape. She hadn't been eating properly lately since she was working after school and fast food had become her best friend. Unfortunately, if she wanted to get into her cheerleader uniform she needed to shed the twelve pounds she'd recently gained. On this morning, she put her headphones in her ears and when the smooth sound of the R&B group Mint Condition caressed her ears she started jogging down the trail.

Fifteen minutes into her run she came upon a familiar physique, bringing a smile to her face.

"Hey Levar, what are you doing out here so early?" she asked.

He smiled and gave her a friendly hug.

"I brought my sister and her teammates out here to practice for an upcoming double Dutch competition."

Denim looked over at the three girls who were engrossed in their routine.

"And this is my girlfriend, Kyra Simmons. Kyra, this is Denim Mitchell. She works over at the clinic with me."

Kyra slid off the hood of Levar's car so she could get a good look at the female who had embraced *her man*.

"Nice to meet you," Kyra replied as she held out her hand to shake Denim's.

Denim shook Kyra's hand and then turned back to Levar.

"So which one of the girls out there is your sister?"

He pointed at Tiffany and said, "The one in the Tennessee Titans jersey."

"Oh, she's pretty. She looks like you," Denim pointed out.

Kyra continued to stare at Denim to size her up. She wasn't sure if she was competition but she could definitely see that she was pretty and that she had a great body under the purple wind suit she was wearing. It was also obvious that Levar was very comfortable with her.

"If you got a minute I'll call them over so you can meet them."

She put her hands up and said, "Oh, I don't want to interrupt their practice. They're really into it."

"It's no big deal. They could use a break. Tiffany! You and your crew come over here for a second!" he yelled.

The three teens ran over to where Levar, Kyra, and an unfamiliar girl were standing.

"What's up, Levar?" Tiffany asked.

"I want you to meet a friend of mine, Denim Mitchell. She works at the clinic with me."

Tiffany smiled and said, "Hi."

Levar pointed to the other girls and said, "These two young ladies are Tiffany's BFFs, Anisa and Laurinda."

In unison, they both greeted Denim with a warm "hello."

"Can we get back to practice now?" Tiffany asked Levar.

He looked at his watch and said, "You have thirty more minutes and then we'll have to leave."

"Okay, it was nice meeting you, Denim," Tiffany replied before they returned to the basketball court to practice.

Denim leaned against the side of Levar's car and watched the trio routine for a few minutes.

"They're good. How did they learn to move like that?" she asked.

Before Levar could answer, Kyra said, "They've been a team for a couple of years now and have won a lot of trophies and ribbons."

"I can see why too," Denim answered before she started jogging in place. "Well, I have to go before my muscles cool down. It was nice meeting you, Kyra."

"You too," Kyra replied as she threw up her hand.

"Levar, I'll see you at work on Monday. Have a great weekend," she yelled before jogging off down the trail.

Minutes into her jog, she was joined by Dré.

"Hey you," she greeted him as she took the iPod earplugs out of her ears.

"I thought I asked you not to go jogging alone."

Denim could see by the expression on Dré's face that he wasn't too happy with her.

"Come on Dré, you know I wouldn't come out here unless there were a lot of people on the trail."

"It's not about that. It's about what I asked you not to do. A woman should never go jogging alone."

The couple stopped running for a second so they

could talk. Denim leaned over to catch her breath before apologizing.

"I'm sorry and you're right, I should've waited for you."

He stared at her and tried to erase the vision of her being attacked out of his mind.

"You look good in your shorts," she pointed out, trying to divert his attention.

"Don't try to change the subject."

Denim tugged on his sweatshirt, pulling him closer to her.

"I said I was sorry. I don't like it when you're angry with me."

"Come here," he replied as he pulled her into his arms. "I'm not angry at you. I love you, Denim, and I don't want anything to happen to you."

She looked up into his soft brown eyes and puckered her lips.

"In that case, may I have a kiss?"

Without hesitation he leaned down and kissed her lovingly on the lips.

"Nice! I love the way your lips feel against mine."

She pushed away and said, "Whatever! Now are you going to work out with me or are we going to kiss all morning?"

He put his hand on his chin as if he had a hard decision to make.

"Now which one would I rather do the most? Kiss you or jog? Hmm, I think I'd rather jog."

She playfully punched him in the arm and said, "Funny, Dré. Let's go."

The young lovers turned and jogged off down the trail and deeper into the park.

Dré and Denim had jogged at least a mile before walking back across the park.

"That felt good, but I can tell I need to work out more often," Denim stated.

He put his arm around her waist and said, "You did good to be out of shape."

"I'm not out of shape," she yelled as she jumped on his back so Dré could give her a piggyback ride back to their vehicles.

"Where are you headed when you leave here?" Dré asked as she slid off his back.

She hugged his neck and asked, "Why do you want to know? Do you have something in mind?"

He opened her car door for her and said, "I can think of a few things I'd like to do. Follow me over to my house."

"Are your parents at home?" she asked as she slid behind the steering wheel and turned on the ignition.

He leaned into the window of the car and said,

"They were when I left but my mom was getting ready to go to work. I don't know about my dad."

"Dré," she called out to him. "I'm not going to mess around with you while your parents are home."

He smiled, showing her his handsome dimples.

"Why not? You've done it before."

"I know, but I was terrified the whole time. I'm not doing that again."

He winked and said, "Don't worry, sweetheart, I got you. Besides, I'll be gentle."

"That's what I'm afraid of," she replied before backing out of the parking space. While she was looking forward to some one-on-one time with Dré she wasn't looking forward to getting embarrassed. His soft touch and gentleness always made her lose control. Denim said a small prayer that Dré's parents were not home as she followed him out the park to his house.

Chapter Five

Upon entering Dré's house, they could smell the aroma of bacon radiating from the kitchen. When they entered the room, they found his dad in the kitchen standing over a sizzling cast-iron skillet full of bacon.

"Good morning, Denim."

"Good morning, Mr. Patterson," she replied.

"Where have you two been?" Garrett asked as he eyed the two.

Dré pulled his sweatshirt over his head and said, "We went to the park to work out."

"Are you hungry?" Garrett asked.

"No sir, I've already eaten, but thank you," Denim replied.

"What about you, son?"

Dré took a look at the crispy bacon and said, "Not right now, but save me a couple of slices."

"Just a couple?" he asked curiously. "I know you eat more than that."

Dré pinched his midsection and said, "I just worked out, Dad. A couple of slices will be more than enough. I'll probably eat a bowl of oatmeal or something with it."

"Denim, are you sure you don't want any? I cooked plenty."

She smiled and said, "I'm sure, but I would like some water."

Garrett opened the refrigerator and handed Denim a bottle of fresh spring water while Dré grabbed a slice of crispy bacon off the platter and bit into it.

"I knew you couldn't resist my bacon."

"Okay, Dad, save me three slices," Dré replied before pulling a bottle of water out of the refrigerator.

"Denim, take this to my room, I'll be right there."

"It was nice seeing you again, Mr. Patterson."

"You too, Denim," Garrett answered as he watched Denim walk out of the kitchen.

Denim walked down the hallway to Dré's room and sat the water bottle on his nightstand.

"Daddy, if you need me, I'll be in my room."

Without turning around, Garrett called out to his son.

"Yes, sir?" he asked as he turned back to his father.

"Don't do anything stupid."

Dré chuckled and asked, "What are you talking about?"

Garrett turned to his son and pointed the prongs down the hallway.

"I wasn't born yesterday. You know exactly what and who I'm talking about."

His dad was quite familiar with the close love affair his son had with Denim and though he'd never caught them, he was almost sure their home had been used by the couple for a romantic teenage romp. Dré had been lectured many times before about his relationship with Denim so he was used to having these man-to-man conversations with his father.

"It's all good, Dad.

"Don't think you and Denim are going to play around in this house like you're newlyweds."

Dré chuckled and said, "We're just going to hang out for a while."

Garrett put the food on his plate and sat down at the table. After taking a sip of coffee he said, "I was seventeen once so I know what it's like. Your hormones are bouncing off the walls, you have a cute girlfriend, and you're in love, but if you're not careful you'll find yourself in a situation like your friend, DeMario."

Dré's best friend DeMario had become a teenage father and his parents reminded him of it nearly every day.

Dré backed his way out of the kitchen with a huge smile on his face and said, "You're worrying for nothing, Dad. I have everything under control."

Garrett looked up from his plate at said, "I can't tell you how many times I've heard that before."

Dré knew his father was right but and if he found out that they'd already had a pregnancy scare weeks earlier he would probably lecture him a little while longer. The fact was that the young couple had been careless a couple of times so when Denim's cycle was late it sent them into a nervous frenzy. Lucky for them, it was only a scare and they got through the stressful situation to-gether.

"I'll be leaving shortly but I won't be gone long," Garrett informed his son.

"Okay," Dré replied as he finally walked out of the kitchen and down the hallway to his bedroom. There he found Denim sitting on his love seat read-ing a book. He closed the door and sat down be-side her.

"What are you reading?"

She flipped the book over to the front cover and said, "It's called *A Sin and A Shame* by Victoria Christopher Murray. I found it on the coffee table in the family room."

Dré inspected the book and said, "That's my mom's book. She's always reading something."

Denim walked over and laid the book on Dré's nightstand before taking a sip of water.

"Did your dad talk about me after I left the room?"

Dré pulled her down into his lap and immediately kissed her on the lips. Denim melted in his arms as she savored the sweet taste of his mouth.

"No, he talked about *us*. Now give me another kiss."

As the couple kissed, Denim nervously kept a close eye on the door.

"We can't do this, Dré," she said as she tried to stand.

He held her in his lap and put his finger over her lips to silence her.

"Relax. My dad will be leaving shortly so we'll have the house all to ourselves."

"I still don't think we should—"

Dré silenced her words with another soul-stirring kiss. Dré knew exactly how to make her lose control. As his strong hands caressed her soft body she was well on her way to falling apart in his arms. That was until there was a loud knock on his bedroom door.

"Dré!" his father yelled as he pounded on the door.

Denim got out of his lap so fast she tripped over his feet and fell hard onto the floor. Dré quickly helped her up before opening the door to face his father.

"Yes, sir?"

Garrett glanced curiously over Dré's shoulder at Denim, who was now innocently watching TV.

"You know we don't allow closed doors when you have female company,"

"Sorry, Daddy. My bad."

"What was that loud thump?" he asked curiously.

"Denim tripped over my foot."

Garrett turned to walk away but hesitated. He turned back to his son and whispered, "Remember what I said earlier."

Dré patted him on the shoulder and with a mischievous smile said, "I will, Dad."

Garrett put on his jacket before walking down the hallway and out into his garage. Seconds later he pulled out of the driveway and disappeared down the street.

"He's gone," Dré announced to Denim as he sat on the bed and pulled her back into his lap.

She buried her face against his warm neck. The warmth of her breath against his neck sent goose bumps down his arm as he rested his hands on her hips.

"I love you."

She cupped his face and gave him a tender kiss.

"I love you too but this is not happening."

"I thought you were going to hang out with me."

She checked the time on her cell phone and said, "I can't right now. I promised my mom I would go shopping with her."

Dré held her hand in his as she led him out of his room and out onto the front porch.

"In that case, instead of watching movies here do you want to get something to eat later and catch a movie?"

"Sounds good," she replied as she made her way out to her car. "I'll call you later."

Regina moved around in the kitchen gracefully as she fried bacon, eggs, biscuits, and potatoes for Dexter. She tightened the belt on her black silk bathrobe and read the note Levar left on the refrigerator alerting her to the fact that he'd taken Tiffany and friends out to practice and wouldn't be home until after noon. Having the morning alone with Dexter allowed them to spend some quality time alone.

Dexter entered the kitchen and hugged Regina's waist.

"Good morning, sweetheart."

She wrapped her arms around his neck and kissed his welcoming lips.

"Good morning to you too," she replied. "I was hoping to finish cooking before you woke up."

He kissed her neck before releasing her and said, "That's okay. I'll help you. Where are the kids?"

She pointed to the note on the refrigerator and then announced, "Levar took Tiffany and the girls to the park to practice and then he's taking them out to breakfast."

Dexter made his way over to the refrigerator and read Levar's note. He opened the refrigerator and removed the butter.

"He's a good kid, Regina, and a becoming a true man."

"Thank you," she answered proudly as she spooned the eggs onto their plates. "Julius did a great job with him."

Dexter pulled two crystal goblets out of the cabinet, filled them with orange juice, and sat them on the table.

"You had a part in it too, sweetheart. Your husband did do an excellent job with him but you need to give yourself some credit too."

"Thank you, baby. That means a lot to me."

He held her chair out for her and said, "The truth speaks for itself."

She sat down and said, "I can't wait for you to meet the rest of my family and friends at my birthday party."

"I'm looking forward to it myself," he responded as he broke off a piece of bacon and put it in his mouth. "This is good and just the way I like it."

Before enjoying their breakfast, the couple joined hands so Dexter could bless their food.

Tiffany sat quietly in the backseat of the car after Levar dropped Anisa and Laurinda off at home.

Kyra turned to her and asked, "So Tiffany, do you think you guys had a good practice?"

She shrugged her shoulders and said, "I guess."

"Don't worry because I know you guys will win. Your routine is so unique and it's really good."

"Thanks, Kyra," she replied softly.

Levar looked at Tiffany in the rearview mirror and asked, "Are you ready to get some breakfast?"

Confused, she asked, "What are you talking about? I thought you were going on a date."

He chuckled and said, "I am, with two of my favorite women."

A huge smile appeared on Tiffany's face.

"I didn't want to say anything in front of your friends."

Tiffany smiled proudly and remembered that even though Levar was dating Kyra it didn't stop him from pampering her as well.

"Thanks, Levar."

"I'm your brother, Tiff, which means there's nothing I wouldn't do for you. Always remember that. Okay?"

She nodded and said, "okay."

Kyra caressed his arm and said, "Ahh, that is so sweet, baby."

"It's the truth, Kyra. My mother and my sister are my life."

Kyra smiled and looked out the window in silence. He reached over and nudged her leg.

"Don't worry. You're at the top of my list too."

"What about Denim?" Kyra asked.

Levar didn't expect Kyra to be jealous of his new coworker, especially since he hadn't given her any reason to be jealous.

"Denim? What does Denim have to do with this conversation?"

Kyra took a deep breath and said, "Nothing really.

It's just that I didn't know you were working with someone so pretty."

"She is pretty, but once again, what does Denim have to do with this?"

"I just thought—"

"Don't think, Kyra. Denim has a boyfriend and I already have someone special in my life too. Don't start getting jealous on me. She's a friend and coworker, nothing more."

"I'm sorry," Kyra whispered. "It's just that it caught me off guard. I had no idea that you was working with someone like that."

Levar laughed at her admission of jealousy.

"It's not funny, Levar."

"I'm sorry. It's just that I've never seen you act jealous before."

Levar pulled into the IHOP parking lot and put the car in park. He turned to Kyra to speak but before he could get a word out, Tiffany interrupted him.

"Give it a rest already, you two," she said in an agitated tone of voice. "Levar is only into you and honestly he's not smart enough to juggle more than one woman at a time."

He turned to his sister and jokingly said, "I don't know whether to thank you or smack you upside the head."

"*Thank you* will be just fine," Tiffany replied with a big smile on her face. "Now can we eat? I'm starving."

Kyra smiled and then threw herself into Levar's arms and gave him a big kiss.

Tiffany rolled her eyes and said, "I'll get the table."

Chapter Six

Regina's birthday had finally arrived and the house was already full of music, family, and friends. Regina greeted one guest after another with Dexter by her side, including Dexter's best friend, Paul Lindsey.

"Paul, I'm so glad you could make it," Regina greeted him. "Dexter said there was a possibility that you might not make it."

Paul kissed Regina's cheek and said, "Regina, you're looking gorgeous as ever and I wouldn't miss this for the world."

"Thank you, Paul. We're so happy you made it."

"So am I. Thankfully I was able to juggle a few things around so I could be here."

Dexter put his arm around Paul's shoulders and said, "I'm surprised. You're always on fast-forward."

"I have to be in order to make the big bucks," he replied as he patted Dexter on the back.

Regina handed Paul a glass of champagne and asked, "So how's business?"

"As a criminal attorney I don't have to tell you how busy I am with this strained economy."

Dexter held his champagne glass up to him and said, "I'll drink to that. Now go over and grab something to eat. I'll join you in a second so I can introduce you to more of the guests."

Paul took a sip of champagne and said, "Will do."

About that time, Regina's in-laws, Freeman and Belinda Ray, entered the house and happily greeted the couple.

"Granddad!" Tiffany yelled before jumping into her grandfather's arms.

"There's my girl!" he proudly yelled.

Tiffany threw her arms around her grandmother's neck, nearly pulling her to the floor.

"Hey, Grandma!"

"Tiffany, my love, you look beautiful."

"Thank you, Grand."

Belinda pulled Regina to the side so they could talk in private. She was an attractive woman with a short hairstyle, which was silver and black.

"Happy birthday, sweetheart," Belinda said to Regina with a loving kiss to the cheek.

"Thank you so much, Belinda."

The two women hugged each other with endearing love.

"You made Julius so happy. You and the children will forever be a part of our family even though it seems you're about to begin a new journey," Belinda stated as she nodded in Dexter's direction. "We want you to know that if you ever need any-thing—and I mean *anything*—you let us know."

Tears fell out of Regina's eyes as she hugged her mother-in-law once again.

"Thank you, Belinda. I love you guys so much. I don't know where I would be if it wasn't for all your love and support."

"We love you too, sweetheart. Now come on so I can meet this man I've heard so much about."

Levar smiled when he saw Kyra enter the door. He hurried across the room and helped her out of her coat. She had on a navy-blue pantsuit with a light blue blouse.

"You look great, Kyra."

"You look handsome in your black suit too. Is it new?" she asked.

"I don't know why Momma wanted us to dress up. We should've just had a cookout so we could at least have on some comfortable clothes."

She kissed him lovingly on the lips and said, "I love seeing you dressed up and that red tie is hot."

"Just like you," he replied mischievously as he took her by the hand and led her over to the table full of food. Regina and Dexter had the party catered with an abundance of finger food, champagne, and punch.

"Did I tell you I invited Denim and her boyfriend?" he asked as he held a ham and cheese skewer up to her mouth.

"No, you didn't tell me, but it's cool," she said before taking a bite of the food. "This is delicious. I can't believe you guys have all this food."

"Look at this, shrimp cocktail. The sauce if off the hook and those mini–roast beef sandwiches are the bomb."

"I can't wait to sample all of it," Kyra replied as she wiped her mouth with a napkin. Then she pointed across the room and said, "Hey, I think your girl is here."

Levar turned and watched Denim and a very tall young man make their way through the crowd.

"Dang! He's hot," Kyra blurted out. "Is that her boyfriend?"

Levar looked at Kyra with a smirk on his face.

"I guess that's him," Levar admitted. "After your

reaction, maybe I'm the one who should be jealous."

She nuzzled his neck and then kissed his cheek.

"He is fine, but you know I only have eyes for you."

Denim and Dré finally made their way over to where Levar and Kyra were standing.

"Nice party, Levar," Denim said as she greeted him. "Hello, Kyra."

"Hi, Denim, it's nice to see you again. I like your dress."

Denim twirled around to model her red, snug-fitting ensemble, which fell just about the knees and displayed her curvy figure and shapely legs. Tonight she wore her hair wavy and her nails were perfectly manicured.

Denim hugged Dré's waist and said, "Thank you, Kyra. Oh! Excuse my manners. This is my boyfriend, André Patterson. Dré this is Levar Ray and his girlfriend, Kyra. I'm sorry, Kyra, but I can't remember your last name."

Kyra shook Dré's hand and said, "It's Simmons."

Dré shook Kyra's hand and then gave Levar a brotherly handshake.

"Kyra Simmons? I know you. Well, I know of you. You've broken just about every high school record in this area. You're a point guard, right?"

Kyra blushed and said, "Yes, and thanks for the compliment. I've heard of you too. You've broken your share of records too."

Denim interrupted them and said, "Kyra, don't brag on him too much, you might just make his head swell bigger than it already is."

"I see you have jokes," Dré replied. All four of them laughed in unison.

Denim looked around and asked, "Where's your sister, Tiffany?"

Levar scanned the crowd and said, "She's around here somewhere."

Upstairs, Tiffany washed her hands after using the bathroom. When she opened the door to exit she was pushed back inside and a large hand immediately covered her mouth. She was unable to get a look at the person's face but whoever it was quickly turned out the light and locked the door.

With his mouth inches from her ear the raspy voice whispered, "If you scream or tell anybody about this I will kill you, your brother, and slit the throat of your beautiful mother—now don't move," he demanded as his large, cold hand touched her intimately.

With tears streaming down her face and trembling with fear, Tiffany froze. She felt nauseated as the man sexually abused her. His breath smelled of strong alcohol and his breathing was deep and repulsive as he violated the very core of her innocence. Tiffany tried to scream but no sound would come out of her mouth as the stranger committed the heinous assault upon her. Minutes later he kissed the back of her neck and let out a repulsive laugh.

"You are my special angel," he whispered in her ear before opening the door. However, before leaving he reminded her of his threat and this time when he said it, it was even more chilling than the first time.

Once he was gone Tiffany found the strength to lock the door. When she turned on the light she saw an unrecognizable face in the mirror. Her hands were trembling as she removed her clothing and turned on the scalding hot water of the shower. After climbing in she spent what seemed like hours scrubbing away the pain, the filth, and the shame.

When she exited the bathroom in her bathrobe she was startled as she ran into Denim in the hallway.

"Hey, Tiffany. Is that your bathroom? The one downstairs is occupied and I really have to go."

Tiffany lowered her eyes. "Yeah," she answered before walking around her.

Before entering the bathroom, Denim asked, "Why aren't you downstairs at the party?"

Caught off guard and not sure what to say she quickly came up with a lie. "My stomach is upset so I'm going to bed."

"There's a lot of food downstairs. Maybe you ate something that didn't agree with you. Do you want me to get your mom?" Denim asked as she reached over to check her forehead for a fever.

Tiffany flinched and then yelled, "No! I'm fine!"

Confused by Tiffany's outburst, she apologized. "I'm sorry, Tiffany. I didn't mean to—"

Tiffany cut her off and said, "I'm sorry too. I didn't mean to yell at you. I just want to lie down."

Denim was picking up on an uneasy vibe, but she couldn't quite put her finger on the problem.

"Are you okay, Tiffany?" Denim asked out of concern as she took a step toward her.

"I will be. Good night."

Denim watched at Tiffany disappeared into what appeared to be her bedroom so she used the bathroom and then rejoined Dré and the rest of the guests downstairs.

* * *

On the drive home, Dré noticed that Denim was quiet. He looked over at her and asked, "Why are you so quiet?"

"I'm sorry, I was just thinking about the party."

"It was nice, wasn't it," he admitted. "Levar seems like a cool guy. The food was off the hook and I'll have to admit I had a good time. I'm glad you invited me to go along."

Denim was silent.

"Cocoa princess, are you listening to me?"

She reached over and touched his arm lovingly.

"Yes, baby, I'm listening to you."

Dré pulled up to the red light at the intersection and smiled. His mind was taking him into the future. A future he couldn't wait to spend with the young woman sitting next to him.

"I can't wait to marry you," he announced

"Really?" she asked.

He glanced over at her and said, "I would never lie about that. I love you."

Denim leaned over and gave Dré a sensual kiss on the lips.

"I can't wait to be with you too, baby."

The light turned green and then there was silence between them once again.

"What's wrong, Denim? You haven't been this quiet in a long time."

She sighed and said, "I'm sorry. I guess I'm just tired. I promise I'll be more talkative tomorrow."

What she was really distracted about was Tiffany and her behavior in the hallway. It was weighing heavy on her mind and even though she'd only met her once, she sensed something was upsetting her more than a stomachache. Maybe in time she could get to know her better and make sure she was really okay. After giving Dré a loving kiss good night she made her way up to her room where she made a short entry into her diary.

Dear Diary,

Dré was my date to a party at Levar's house tonight. It was his mother's birthday and the food was off da hook. I had a strange encounter with his sister and it's really bothering me. I hope to find out why she was acting so weird. Dré looked hot as usual and my heart is running over with love for him.

Later,

D

On the other side of town Regina gave Tiffany two teaspoons of Pepto-Bismol.

"I'm sorry you don't feel well, sweetheart."

She forced a smile and said, "I'll be okay, Momma."

"I don't feel right leaving you," she revealed. "Maybe we should stay here tonight."

"Don't change your plans because of me. Besides, Levar is here."

Regina paced the floor and said, "I never left you guys when you were sick and I'm not about to do it now. Dexter will understand if we stay."

"Momma, if you don't go I'll feel guilty."

Dexter walked into the room, startling Tiffany.

"Is everything okay in here? Tiffany, how are you feeling?" he asked as he approached the bed.

"I'll be fine if you guys would just go so I can get back to sleep. I said I was fine."

He looked at Regina and whispered, "Maybe we should stay."

"That's exactly what I was thinking," she replied.

"Momma, you already have your bag packed. Go, I'm okay. Good night."

She leaned down and kissed her forehead. "It's out of the question. We're staying here. Understood?"

"Understood," she repeated.

Regina walked toward the hallway and said, "If you need me I'll be down the hallway."

"I hope you feel better, Tiffany," Dexter said as he reached down and caressed her cheek.

She turned away from him, causing him to frown. He stared at her in disbelief before walking out of her room and down the hallway to Regina's room.

Chapter Seven

Levar exited the school and hurried through the parking lot to his car.

Kyra called out to him just before he opened the car door. When she finally made her way through the cars and students she said, "Hey stranger."

"Hey yourself. What's up?"

She put her hands on her hips and replied, "You tell me. I think I've only seen you about ten minutes since your mom's birthday party last weekend."

Levar lowered his head and softly replied, "I know and I'm sorry. I've been busy."

Kyra leaned against the car and said, "I have basketball practice every day but I still take time to text you."

He pulled her into his arms and said, "You're right and I'm sorry."

A slight smile appeared on Kyra's face as she forgave him. Not that he thought she wouldn't anyway.

"Apology accepted." She put her arm around his waist and announced, "You have a lot of making up to do with me."

He hugged her lovingly and said, "I think I can arrange that."

She released him and said, "Perfect. I have to get to practice but I hope to see you later."

"No doubt," he replied before climbing into his car and driving out of the parking lot.

Across town at Langley High, Denim sat under a large oak tree and scanned over the results of a test in her honors chemistry class. Her prize was a well-deserved A on the top of the page. Denim had studied extra hard for the test and couldn't wait to show her parents. A few of her classmates was disappointed in their grades but the teacher assured them they would have a chance to redeem themselves. Moments later she checked the time and quickly grabbed their belongings, but before she could take one step, Dré, who was normally in the gym getting ready for basketball practice, hugged her from behind.

Startled, she looked over her shoulders and asked, "Why aren't you at practice?"

"I'm going in a second. Coach is in a meeting so we have a little time to hang out."

"Look. I got an A on my chemistry test," she replied with excitement as she held the paper up for him to see it.

He looked at her paper and then rewarded her with a soft kiss on the lips.

"Congratulations, baby," he whispered. "Colleges are going to be kicking down your door."

Denim hugged Dré's waist and said, "Thank you."

He leaned down and kissed her once again and said, "I would love it if you would let me properly reward you on your A."

Denim blushed as Dré's hand slid down her back to her curvy backside.

"You know I love your rewards and I wish I could hang out with you a little longer, but I have to go to work."

Seconds later, a teacher disciplined the young couple for their public display of affection, causing Dré to reluctantly remove his hand from Denim's hips.

"Busted," Denim joked as they passed the teacher and made their way over to her car.

"I'm not thinking about that teacher," Dré replied as he looked over his shoulder and pulled Denim back into his arms and kissed her again, leaving her breathless.

"You keep that up, Prime Time, and you're going to get us both in school suspension."

He leaned down close to her ear and whispered, "You're worth it."

Denim shivered for the warmth of his breath on her skin.

"I'll see you later. Have fun at work," he announced as he slowly backed away from her.

"I will and when I get off work I might just swing by your house to get that reward," she replied before putting her book bag in the truck of her car. Dré stood in the middle of the parking lot in a daze until one of his teammates ran by and tossed him a basketball. As Dré dribbled the basketball toward the gym, he hoped to get the chance to spend some quality time with Denim even if it was only a brief encounter.

Denim sat her purse on the passenger seat and then pulled out her diary to jot down a few thoughts.

Dear Diary,
   I got an A on my chemistry test. Yay!! I'm so psyched for the next one and hope I get an A on my biology test as well. On a personal

note, Dré is driving me crazy. My heart beats like crazy when I'm around him and when he touches and kisses me, I lose it. I honestly believe this is what loves feels like and I never want it to end. I'm headed to work and I hope to talk to Levar about his sister. She's still heavy on my mind but hopefully she's doing better than the last time I saw her.
Later,
D

Regina stepped outside of her office building and was immediately met with the heat of the afternoon sun. The forecast had been the same for several days and she couldn't wait for a cool relief. While the weather didn't affect her job, the hot weather made life on the construction site a lot more exhausting for Dexter and his crew. However, he actually welcomed the heat over a rainy day since it usually caused delays that could cost him thousands of dollars. Luckily for him, by starting work before the crack of dawn it had actually allowed him to get ahead of schedule.

Dexter looked at his watch and pulled out his cell to call Regina.

"Hello?" she answered as she opened her car door.

"Hey, sweetheart, are you off work?" he asked.

"You bet. I'm just getting to my car. How was your day?"

He looked out over the city and said, "It was perfect. I'm twenty-six floors off the ground and I'm looking at a breathtaking view of the city."

"I'm sure it is beautiful. How are you dealing with the heat?" she asked as she turned on the air conditioner.

"It's actually a nice breeze blowing up here," he replied as he inspected a steel beam that his workers were about to weld. "Besides, I'm used to it."

"Are you coming over for dinner tonight?" she asked as she lowered the volume on her stereo.

"I don't know about tonight. I have to be here late and then I have to go check the progress on one of my other sites."

"You're a busy man, Mr. Banks."

"I'm trying to make that money, baby."

"I know, just make sure you be careful. I don't want you to get hurt."

"Always, sweetheart."

"Well, I'll talk to you later. When I get home I have to take the girls out to that park to practice with those crimpers."

Dexter laughed out loud.

"It's krumpers, babe, not crimpers. I thought you were hip."

She also laughed and said, "I am hip—at least I think I am."

"You're hip enough for me. Listen, sweetheart, if I finish early I'll try to get by there a little later. I love seeing you after a crazy day at work. You always know how to calm me."

"You calm me too."

Dexter made his way over to the construction elevator and closed the gate. He pushed the button for the ground floor and then began to reveal something to her that he'd been holding in for some time.

"Regina, I have something to confess to you."

"What's that, babe?" she asked.

He swallowed the lump in his throat and said, "You make me feel all sorts of wonderful things and I'd like to make things more permanent between us, but I don't know how the kids would feel about it."

Regina felt like the wind was knocked out of her. Was Dexter asking her what she thought he was asking her? She didn't want to get ahead of herself, but she did want to clarify exactly what he was saying.

"Regina? Are you still there?" he asked.

She cleared her throat and said, "I'm here."

"I want you to know that this is not the way I'd planned on asking you, but—"

"What exactly are you asking me, Dexter?" she asked as her heartbeat sped up.

He smiled and then said, "Hold that thought. I'm a gentleman and my mom and dad taught me better manners than this. I'll see you at six-thirty."

"I thought you had to work late?" she asked.

His baritone voice chuckled on the other end of the telephone.

"Never mind that. I love you, Regina, and I love the kids. I'll see you at six-thirty."

"I love you too. See you soon," she replied before hanging up.

Could this be a marriage proposal from Dexter? she thought as she clutched her cell phone. He was a handsome, sexy, and wealthy man, but why would he really want to marry her with two children? Also, if it was a marriage proposal what would the children think about it? The thought of them not approving scared her because she didn't want them to think she was trying to replace their father. She had loved her husband with all her heart and losing him was the worst thing she'd ever experienced, but she was in love with Dexter and wanted to spend the rest of her life with him.

* * *

Later that evening, Dexter showed up on Regina's doorstep at sixty-thirty as promised. When he ar-rrived they didn't pick up where they left off; instead, he helped her prepare dinner. Tiffany was in her room doing homework and Levar was still at work.

"I have something for you," Dexter whispered into Regina's ear as he chopped up onions and garlic.

Blushing, she asked, "You do? What is it?"

He winked at her right before he poured some olive oil in a hot skillet and then added the onions, celery, and garlic to the pan.

"After dinner. Okay?" he whispered lovingly into her ear.

"Okay," she answered nervously while pulling a pan of hot rolls out of the oven. She poured two glasses of red wine and then watched at he added the grilled chicken and some seasonings to the mixture.

Regina leaned over the skillet to inhale the va-pors.

"Baby, that smells so good. You really know your way around the kitchen."

"I'm a bachelor, I have to know how to cook if I want to eat, plus my mother made sure I learned how to cook. She wouldn't have had it any other way."

She took a sip of wine and said, "You can afford to eat out everyday if you wanted to."

He grabbed his stomach and said, "Yeah, if want a pot belly, but I don't."

"I'll drink to that," she added as she lovingly caressed his chest.

Dexter kissed her on the lips and said, "You have a sensational body yourself. Most twenty-year-olds should be jealous of you."

"Thank you, baby, but I wouldn't go that far," she replied as she glanced over at the chicken.

"You know I'm telling the truth," he answered as he removed the chicken and placed it on a platter.

Dexter's statement warmed her heart as she set the table with a huge smile on her face. Minutes later, Regina called Tiffany down to dinner and the three of them sat down and enjoyed their delicious meal.

Once dinner was over and the kitchen was clean Dexter presented Regina with a small gold box adorned with a gold bow. Inside the decorative box was a two-karat, emerald-cut diamond ring with rows of diamonds on the band. He happily slid it onto her left hand and said, "Regina, I love you. Will you marry me?"

Tears filled her eyes as she stared down at the ring and then into his eyes. She was so happy she was unable to speak, so she nodded her answer instead. As she hugged his neck, Dexter held her close to his heart. Now all they had to do was get the approval of Levar, who was at work, and Tiffany, who was still struggling to accept the loss of her dad.

Later that night, Regina sat with Levar and broke the news to him about her engagement. "You're getting married?" Levar asked.

Regina fumbled with her response after showing her son the engagement ring.

"Son, I love Dexter and he loves me too."

Levar held his head in his hands in disbelief. His mother's relationship with Dexter seemed like it was moving on fast-forward.

Regina put her hand on her son's shoulders and asked, "Does this mean you're against me marrying Dexter?"

"You haven't been dating him that long, Momma. What's the big rush to get married?"

"I'm not rushing," Regina explained as she turned off the light in the kitchen and then walked back into the family room and sat down. "I've been dating Dexter for almost nine months. I dated your father only four months before I married him."

"I didn't know," Levar revealed.

Regina smiled and caressed her son's cheek and said, "There's a lot you don't know, son."

Levar listened attentively as his mother spoke.

"I know when it's true love, Levar. I knew it was love when I met your father and I know it's love with Dexter. Can't you trust my judgment?"

"I do trust you, but—"

She cut him off before he could finish his sentence.

"Sweetheart, when I met your father it was love at first sight. I loved him for nineteen beautiful years. He's been gone for two years now. How long is long enough?"

Regina went on to tell her son that she was only seventeen years old when she first met his father during her senior year in high school. They became close friends and remained friends throughout college but didn't start dating seriously until four months before their graduation. She explained to him that it was love at first sight for her but she didn't want to risk damaging their great friendship, so she concealed her feelings for him. Finally, four months before their graduation the couple confessed their true love for each other and started dating seriously. Julius proposed to her the week before graduation and they got married a month later. Less than a year later, Levar was born.

Levar lowered his head and asked, "Does Tiffany know about the engagement?"

"I wanted to talk to you first."

Levar studied his mother's facial expression.

"I'm not saying I'm totally against you marrying Dexter," he explained as he sat down beside her. "I just don't want you to get hurt."

"I've given this a lot of thought and I'd told myself that if Dexter loved me like I loved him and he ever asked me to marry him, I'd say yes, but if you and Tiffany are against it I'll have to rethink it. You two are the most important people in my life and I want you to be happy too."

Levar thought about his father and how their happiness was one thing he was adamant about.

"If you believe that Dexter is the man to make you happy, Momma, then go for it."

"Do you mean it?" She asked and then held her breath.

"Yes, ma'am. It's cool."

Regina smiled and then kissed Levar on the cheek.

"Thank you, son, and I want you to know this is not just about me being happy. I want you and Tiffany to be happy too. I just hope she approves."

Levar stood and swung his book bag on his shoulder. "I don't think Tiffany is going to be against it.

She still misses Daddy and she seems to like Dexter, especially since he's been helping her with the double Dutch competition."

"I hope you're right, Levar. Tiffany, like most girls, was a daddy's girl and his death devastated her."

"It devastated all of us," he reminded her before leaning down to kiss his mother's forehead. "Good night. I'll see you in the morning."

Regina stood and hugged her son tightly. "I love you, Levar," she whispered.

"I love you too," he replied before making his way out of the room and toward the stairs. The news of his mother's engagement weighed heavy on his mind as he climbed the stairs. He wondered how his paternal grandparents were going to take the news. While they'd remained very close to them since the death of their father, would they accept his mother marrying Dexter? He had a headache now and didn't want to think about it anymore because he had a history assignment to finish before going to bed.

In the shadows of the upstairs hallway, Tiffany backed away from the railing after eavesdropping on the conversation between her brother and mother.

She had gotten out of bed only because she heard Levar's car pull into the garage. Before he had arrived home she had obtained the courage to tell him about the assault, but after hearing the conversation about the engagement she changed her mind. Her mother was marrying Dexter and it looked like he was going to be her stepfather after all. It made her feel a little weird after her conversation with Anisa and Laurinda. What was this going to mean for them? Would they have to move? Would she have to go to a new school and make new friends? Would her mother be having more children? Hopefully not, but Dexter didn't have kids and he might want some.

Levar entered his room and turned on the light. It startled him to find Tiffany sitting in a chair in the corner of the room with only the moonlight shining in from the window. By the look on her face he could tell something was wrong.

"Hey Tiffany, what are you doing sitting in here in the dark?"

"Waiting for you," she answered.

Levar dropped his book bag on the floor and studied his sister.

"What's up?"

She let out a breath and said, "You tell me."

Levar sat his keys on his nightstand and said, "I guess you heard, huh?"

She folded her arms and said, "I heard some of it."

He looked his sister in the eyes and said, "Then you know they're getting married?"

"When?" she asked.

"I don't know, but it'll probably be soon. They're always together anyway."

Tiffany thought about the unknown future ahead of them with Dexter and said, "If Momma wants to marry Dexter, fine, but if they have kids, I'm not babysitting."

Levar chuckled and said, "You're getting a little ahead of yourself, aren't you?"

"Am I?" she asked. "He doesn't have kids and you know he's going to want some now."

"It'll be okay, sis, and if Momma and Dexter have kids, I'm sure they'll be just as sweet as you are."

Levar's statement made Tiffany smile. At that moment she felt like telling him her darkest secret once again.

"Levar?"

"Yes?" he asked as he released her and then picked up his cell phone to respond to a text message from Kyra.

The words were on the tip of her tongue but she was unable to force them out. The pain still consumed her body and no matter how hard she prayed when she closed her eyes, she could still hear the man's voice, feel his body, and smell his breath. It was all too vivid for her so she jumped out of her seat and ran for the door.

"Tiffany? Where are you going?" he asked as he grabbed her arm. "I thought you wanted to tell me something."

"I don't feel so good, Levar. I have to go to the bathroom."

Levar put his cell phone down and felt her head.

"You don't have a fever, but your eyes don't look so good. Is it your stomach again?"

All she wanted to do was get to the bathroom. She was nauseated and could feel her stomach attempting to betray her.

"Yeah, but I'll be okay. I just need to get the bathroom," she announced.

He kissed her on the cheek and said, "Go ahead, but if you need me, let me know. We'll talk more tomorrow. Good night, Tiff."

"Good night, Levar."

Levar hoped his sister wasn't suffering from a stomach virus. She'd been under the weather off and on for a couple of weeks now, but maybe the news of their mother's engagement was the culprit upsetting her tonight. What Levar didn't know was there was more to Tiffany's illness than he could ever imagine and once the secret was out it would nearly kill him and his entire family.

Regina retired to her bedroom to call Dexter. When he picked up the telephone he sounded very tired.

"Hey baby. I'm sorry, did I wake you?" she asked.

He smiled upon hearing her voice and said, "No, I'm still up."

"Listen, sweetheart, I know you're tired but I wanted to call to let you know that I told Levar about our engagement."

"How did he take it?" he asked as he poured himself a glass of wine and unbuttoned his shirt.

"I think he was shocked, but we talked and he eventually admitted that he only wanted me to be happy."

"But he's really against it, huh?"

"No, he's not against it. His only concern is he thinks we're moving too fast."

He took a sip of the wine and said, "You did tell him that I'm not trying to replace their father, right?"

"He knows that, babe. He just doesn't want me to get hurt."

"I'd never hurt you, Regina," he said softly into the phone.

"I know that," she admitted to him. "Levar is very protective of me and Tiffany."

Dexter chuckled. "And he should be. Do you mind if I talk to him?"

"Of course I don't, and while Tiffany adores you, she still has days when she misses her father terribly."

"It was a tragic accident, Regina. The kids are still traumatized. I know you are too, but I hope to take all your pain and sadness away. I really do love you and I want to take care of you and the kids."

"That's so sweet of you and I love you too. We'll get through this and so will the kids."

Chapter Eight

"Levar! What are you doing?" Denim yelled as she turned off the treadmill so Levar's patient could get off.

"What?" he replied excitably as he finally snapped back to reality.

"I'm so sorry, Mr. Green. Are you okay?" he asked as he helped the sixty-something gentleman from the treadmill.

He patted Levar on the shoulder and said, "It's okay, son. I needed the extra minutes anyway."

Denim also apologized to Mr. Green before instructing him to go over to Tony to finish up the rest of his exercises. Once the patient was out of hearing distance, Levar turned to Denim and said, "Denim, I'm sorry, I didn't hear you calling me."

She wiped down the treadmill with disinfectant

and asked, "What's going on with you today? You're distracted and that's not good when you're working with patients."

Levar lowered his head and said, "It's personal."

Denim motioned for him to follow her down the hallway. They entered the spa room and sat down.

"Listen, Levar, we all have personal things going on but you can't bring it in here, so whatever you have going on you need to leave it at the door."

He put his head in his hands and said, "That's easier said than done."

"Do you want to talk about it?" Denim asked as she grabbed a handful of towels.

Levar hesitated for a moment and then decided to share his problem with his coworker and new friend.

"My mom got engaged last night."

"That's great," Denim replied with a smile. "I'm happy for your mother. Aren't you?"

"The jury is still out on that one because I don't know how to feel."

Denim sat the towels on a massage table and asked, "You don't know? Why don't you know?"

He was silent and Denim wasn't sure if she should push him but she decided to do it anyway.

"If you talk about it you might feel better. You

can trust me. I really am a good listener and what's said in the spa room stays in the spa room," she joked.

Levar took a breath and then looked into Denim's eyes.

"My dad was killed in a car accident a couple of years ago and I haven't gotten over it. It seems weird seeing my mom with a boyfriend."

She reached over and took his hand. "I'm so sorry about your dad, Levar, I didn't know."

He smiled and said, "I know you didn't. My dad was everything to us and we lost him in the blink of an eye. I just think it's too soon for my mom to get married again, that's all."

"Do you like the guy?" Denim asked.

"He's cool."

Denim could see that Levar was holding back his true feelings, so she realized she would have to approach him a difference way.

"Okay, let me ask you something. What is it about your mom's fiancé that you don't like? Is he disrespectful to your mom? Is he abusive, a dead-beat, or an alcoholic? Does he yell at you and your sister? Mistreat you?"

Levar chuckled and realized what Denim was doing.

"I get your point and to answer your questions,

no, he's none of those things, but how can I know he's shown me his true personality?"

"You don't, you just have to pray, Levar, and trust your mom's instincts. She married your dad and that was a good thing. This one could be a great thing too."

"I know she's been lonely and I know she misses my dad too," he answered as he stood. "Maybe you're right and I'm freaking out for no reason."

"Are you saying you *never* expected your mom to fall in love again?"

"To be honest, no, I didn't. I mean, I kind of expected her to date but not bring another man into my father's house."

Denim shook her head in disbelief.

"Are you listening to yourself? Wasn't it your mom's house too? You men are a trip!" she yelled as she stood and started forcefully placing the towels in the cabinet above the massage table. Levar could see that Denim was somewhat agitated with him now.

"Let me ask you something, Levar. What if it had been your mom that passed away? Would you not expect your dad fall in love again and remarry and possibly bring another woman into your mother's house?"

Frustrated, he yelled, "I don't know! All I know

is my family has been ripped apart and now this stranger is coming into our lives to possibly change everything."

"Have you ever considered that things could change for the better? This man might just be the breath of fresh air all of you need after experiencing such a horrible thing."

He stared at the floor in silence. Denim had made a great point and it was one he hadn't thought about. Maybe Dexter was a blessing to him and his family that he wasn't able to see yet.

Denim touched his arm tenderly and said, "Give it time, Levar. I'm sure things will work out between you and your new stepfather, but you're going to have to keep your head on straight if you're going to work here. You can't forget about the patients because all it takes is one second of negligence and someone could get hurt."

"I'm sorry," he replied softly. "I didn't mean to neglect Mr. Green."

She linked her arm with his and said, "Apology accepted. Mr. Green needed those extra minutes on the treadmill anyway. Just remember that I'm on your side. Levar, you're on the road to being a great therapist. Don't screw it up."

"I won't," he replied as he gave her an appreciative hug.

Denim stepped out of his embrace and said, "Great! Now what's going on with Tiffany?"

"That's another thing. I can't put my finger on it but she's not herself and she keeps complaining about her stomach."

"Have you asked her what was bothering her?" Denim asked as she set the exam table up for the next patient.

"No, but if something was really wrong, she'd tell me. We always tell each other everything."

"That's great, Levar, but it still wouldn't hurt to ask her. Girls are like that."

"I will." He helped Denim ready the exam room.

"I'm sure things will work out with your mom and Tiffany. If you ever want to talk, I'm here. Now we better get back to work before Tony comes looking for us."

They walked out into the hallway together and back into the therapy room.

Regina and Dexter sat across the table from Tiffany and waited for a reaction. Instead she stuck a couple of French fries into her mouth.

"Tiffany, did you hear what I said? We're getting married."

Tiffany took a sip of Sprite and then said, "I heard you the first time, Momma."

Dexter chuckled before speaking.

"Well, do you have anything to say about it?" Dexter asked Tiffany. "We want to know if you're okay with me marrying your mother."

Tiffany looked at her mother and then over at Dexter and frowned.

"What if I did have a problem with it?" she said in funky tone of voice. "Would it make a difference? You guys are only asking me so you won't feel guilty. You're going to get married whether I'm okay with it or not."

"Watch your tone with me, young lady," Regina scolded her loudly, causing a few patrons to look in their direction. "You can disagree with me without getting an attitude. What is wrong with you? You've been acting so mean lately. I've been letting you get away with it but not anymore."

Dexter put his hands up and said, "Can we all take a deep breath for a minute, please?"

Mother and daughter sat in silence for a few seconds before Tiffany apologized and said, "I'm sorry, Momma."

"You should be," she replied as she shifted in her seat. "You know I don't allow you to talk to me like that."

"Okay," Momma, I said I was sorry."

Regina's eyes were beginning to tear up. She

was expecting to have a sensible conversation with her daughter but what she was getting was a lot of attitude.

"Momma, you guys asked me what I thought about you getting married. Okay, Dexter, you're cool but I really don't know how it's going to make me feel."

Dexter smiled and asked, "Are you against it?"

Tiffany took a deep breath before answering. She could see the anxiety in their faces as if their whole future depended on her answer.

Tiffany looked Dexter in the eyes and said, "I still cry for my daddy, so if you guys get married it's going to take time for me to get used to you being around the house."

"I understand," he replied as he tenderly touched her hand. "I'm not trying to replace your dad. From what I heard about him he was a good man and a great father."

Tiffany quickly pulled her hand away, drawing her mother's attention. Dexter's hand was large and rough like the man who had assaulted her.

"Tiffany, what's going on with you?" her mother asked.

With her hands in her lap the nauseated feeling had returned.

"I need to go to the restroom," she announced.

"Do you want me to go with you?" her mother asked.

"No!" she yelled, completely out of character.

Regina studied her and agreed to let her go to the restroom alone. It was there that Tiffany's lunch came up.

Out at the table Regina put her hands over her face and said, "What's wrong with my daughter? She's never acted like this."

"This is a big deal to the kids, Regina. I expected a little resistance."

Tiffany returned to the table and took a sip of her soda.

"Are you feeling okay, Tiffany?" she asked.

"I'm fine, Momma."

Dexter motioned for the waitress to bring the check.

"You don't look well, Tiffany. Let's get you home."

Tiffany rolled her eyes and then said, "But we haven't finished our food."

"We can finish it at home," Dexter added as he pulled out his credit card and handed it to the waitress. "Also could you bring us some carryout containers for our food?"

"I sure can. I'll be right back with your receipt," the waitress replied before walking away.

"Thanks for dinner, Dexter," Regina said softly.

He kissed her cheek and said, "It's my pleasure."

Tiffany sat silently as they waited for the waitress to return. She looked at her mother and Dexter and said, "I'm sorry I ruined dinner."

Dexter smiled and placed a ten-dollar bill on the table to tip the waitress.

"You didn't ruin dinner, sweetheart. I can tell you don't feel well. I just hope that you and Levar give me a chance. I love you guys and your mother very much and I promise to take care of you like you were my own children."

Tiffany thought to herself as she stared into Dexter's eyes, searching for his sincerity. He didn't blink or look away, which was usually a sign that someone was lying. After a few more seconds, she realized that Dexter was being truthful.

She took a breath and said, "I guess it would be cool after all if you guys got married, so I vote yes."

Regina had been holding her breath. She finally took a breath and leaned over the table to hug her daughter.

"Thank you, Tiffany. I love you and I promise I will never do anything to shame or dishonor your father's memory."

"Okay. When do you plan to get married?" Tiffany asked.

Regina looked at Dexter and said, "We haven't talked about a date yet."

"How do you feel about a Christmas wedding? It's only three months away and I could be a bridesmaid."

Dexter clapped his hands together and said, "That sounds good to me. What about you, sweetheart?"

Regina stuttered for a minute and then agreed as she kissed Dexter lovingly. The waitress returned with Dexter's credit card, receipt, and their carry-out containers.

"On that note, let's get out of here," Dexter announced as he stood and tucked his billfold in his back pocket.

Minutes later the three of them walked out of the restaurant and into the parking lot to his awaiting vehicle. Tiffany was onboard with the couple; now Dexter needed to talk to Levar man-to-man to make sure he would accept him marrying Regina during the Christmas holidays. Little did they know, Tiffany was dealing with her own hell and it was eating her from the inside and out.

Levar arrived home thirty minutes after Regina, Dexter, and Tiffany returned from the restaurant.

Since Levar couldn't join them for dinner they'd brought him his favorite meal, chicken tenders with honey-mustard sauce and fries. After finishing off the last piece of chicken, Levar sat down next to Dexter, who had challenged him in playing the PlayStation 3 NFL game. Regina and Tiffany had gone up to bed, leaving the two men alone to talk. Levar admired Dexter for the fact that while he worked on and around dirty construction sites, he never looked or smelled like he did. It was obvious that he took pride in his appearance.

As Dexter punched the buttons to run a play on Levar's team, he asked, "How the new job working out with school?"

"It's all good," Levar answered as he pressed a series of buttons on his controller.

"Are you still dating that young lady, what's her name?"

"Her name is Kyra."

"Yeah, that's it. Are you guys—"

"Why are you cross-examining me?" Levar asked.

Dexter smiled and said, "My bad. I didn't mean to pry. I'm just interested in what's going on in your life."

Now it was Levar's time to laugh.

"What's really on your mind, Dexter?"

"I'm that transparent, huh?" he asked.

"Yes, you are."

"Okay," I'll stop beating around the bush. What I really want to know is if it would be okay with you if I married your mother around Christmas?"

Without skipping a beat, Levar replied, "What do you mean *around* Christmas?"

"You know, maybe on the twenty-seventh or twenty-eighth. I definitely don't want it to interfere with the holidays."

Levar glanced over at Dexter and said, "Good, because we usually spend Christmas with my grandparents."

"Do you mean your father's parents or your mother's parents?" he asked.

"Both, but since my dad died we spend a lot more time with my dad's parents," Levar revealed.

"I see," he answered. "You know, me and your mother went to visit them today so she could tell them about our engagement."

Levar stopped playing for a second and asked, "How did it go?"

Dexter put the game on pause and turned to Levar.

"They took the news well, considering I'm marrying their daughter-in-law. I expected it to be difficult for them but we were able to talk about it and in the end they gave us their blessings. So did Regina's parents."

Levar nodded without speaking.

"You know, your grandparents love you guys very much and their main concern is that you're loved and that I take care of you guys just like their son did."

With a somewhat solemn but agreeable tone, Levar replied, "I know."

"Now, I was kind of worried about your sister's response to the news and she had us going for awhile, and then she was the one who suggested that we have the wedding around Christmas."

Once again, Levar was silent. Dexter put his hand on Levar's shoulder and said, "Levar, you know both sets of your grandparents are good people and I'm going to do everything in my power to live up to all your expectations."

Levar looked his future stepfather in the eyes and said, "I'm counting on it. Don't let me down."

"I won't," he answered proudly as he removed his hand and started playing the game once again.

Levar and Dexter continued to play the video game for another hour before retiring to bed.

Upstairs, Regina turned over and snuggled up to Dexter as he climbed into bed.

"Is everything okay?" she asked softly.

"Everything's just fine, baby," he answered as he wrapped his arm around her warm body and closed his eyes.

Chapter Nine

The next morning, Tiffany got up bright and early. She was supposed to practice with her team but she wasn't feeling it. When Laurinda and Anisa arrived to practice, she broke the unexpected news to them that she was quitting the team.

"Quitting?" Laurinda asked with her hands on her hips.

Tiffany sat down on the front porch steps and said, "You heard me. I don't want to do it any more. If you guys still want to go to the competition you can find someone to replace me."

Anisa waved her hands in the air and said, "Wait a minute. Where is all this coming from, Tiffany? You were the main one talking about not stopping until we won nationals. What's changed?"

"Can't I quit if I want to?" Tiffany yelled angrily.

"Hold up!" Laurinda yelled back at her. "I can't

believe you're quitting a few weeks before the competition? This is some bull!"

"Well, believe it," Tiffany replied. "Listen, it's nothing against you guys, I just don't want to jump anymore."

Anisa looked at Tiffany angrily and said, "Forget this! I'm done!"

"What's really going on?" Laurinda gently asked as they watched Anisa walk out of the yard and down the sidewalk. This was not the Tiffany she knew and something had to have drastically changed for her to give up her first love.

Tiffany stood and folded her arms in defiance and softly answered, "I want to do something different, that's all."

Laurinda backed away from her friend and said, "Well, good-bye, Tiffany. I guess we'll see you around."

Tiffany watched as Laurinda slowly walked down her driveway, out of her yard and out of sight.

With everything else going on, now she'd chased her best friends away. As she turned to go into the house she noticed a shiny black Mercedes pulling into the driveway.

"Hey, Tiffany, how are you doing?" Paul Lindsey called out to her as he climbed out of the car.

"I'm fine. What are you doing here?" she asked cautiously.

"Dexter asked me to meet him here," he revealed as he stepped out of the car and approached her. He reached into the pocket of his expensive-looking gray suit and pulled out a pack of gum and held it out to her.

"Want some?"

"No, thanks," she answered with a little attitude as she took a step back from him.

He stuck a piece of gum in his mouth and said, "It's good. You don't know what you're missing."

"Dexter didn't call to say he was coming over and he always calls."

"He didn't?" Paul asked. "Maybe I misunderstood him."

Levar walked out onto the porch and said, "Hello, Mr. Lindsey."

"Please, call me Paul," he replied as he shook Levar's hand.

"What can I do for you?" Levar asked as Tiffany quietly made her way back into the house.

"I was telling Tiffany that Dexter asked me to meet him here."

Levar folded his arms and said, "Well, Dexter don't live here and while my mom's at work, I'm in charge, which means no one can come into our house."

Paul held up his hands and said, "My bad and I

totally understand where you're coming from. Listen, I'm going to give Dexter a call and make sure he cleared everything with Regina. I don't want to cause any problems."

"It doesn't matter because like I said, Dexter doesn't live here," Levar reiterated firmly.

Paul took a step back and then walked back over to his Mercedes. "Calm down, son. It's cool. As a matter of fact, I'll give Dexter a call and let him know I'll meet him at the gym instead. Give your mother my regards and tell Tiffany good-bye."

"Will do," Levar replied as he closed and locked the front door.

Nearly a half hour had passed and Tiffany had spent the time in her room doing homework. Levar entered the room and said, "I just got off the phone with Anisa and Laurinda. They said you quit jump rope. What's going on with you?" he asked tenderly, not wanting to upset her—but it didn't work.

Tiffany slammed her pencil down and said, "I wish everyone would just leave me alone."

She jumped up from her desk and charged past Levar, but he grabbed her arm and asked angrily, "What the hell is wrong with you, Tiff?" "This is not you and I want to know what's wrong right now!"

Tiffany pulled away from him and yelled, "Don't touch me!"

Shocked and in disbelief, he released her arm and followed her out into the hallway.

"Why are you tripping?" he screamed at her. "I don't know what's going on with you but you need to get that attitude of yours in check."

Emotionally spent, Tiffany broke down in tears and apologized to her brother. "I'm sorry, Levar. I didn't mean to yell at you."

"Apology accepted," he quickly answered as he stared at his sister. "You've been acting weird for a while now. I know something's different about you and I wish you would tell me what's wrong."

With tears running down her cheeks she hugged her brother's neck and said, "I'll be okay. I love you, Levar."

Her statement all but confirmed to him that something had gone down. Either Tiffany had witnessed something horrific, heard about it or experienced it. Now his job was to determine which one it was.

"Sis, if something's bothering you, you need to tell me so I can fix it."

"Thank you Levar, but there's nothing you can do to help me."

He grabbed her chin and made her look him in the eyes. "Yes I can and I will if you would just tell me."

Tiffany opened her mouth to speak and the words nearly came out until she saw the frantic look on his face. He was pleading with her with his eyes and Tiffany knew she was torturing him, but the threat of her assailant against her family prevented her from saying the words. Levar could see her pain and decided to regroup.

He hugged her and said, "It's going to be okay, Tiffany. Stop crying. I'm here for you. I know whatever you have to tell me might be bad so just scream out the words so I can take care of it."

She buried her face against his chest and whispered, "I can't."

Levar was furious inside but he had to treat her delicately. His mind was racing with all sorts of crazy thoughts and he hoped his imagination was just that.

An hour later an unexpected visitor arrived on their front porch. When Tiffany opened the door she found Denim standing there with a huge smile on her face.

"Hey Tiffany, how are you doing?"

Tiffany let Denim into the foyer and said, "I'm okay."

"Did you get over your stomachache?" she asked her.

"Yeah, I got over it. I'll get Levar," she replied as she closed the door. "Levar! You have company!"

"Who is it?" he yelled from upstairs.

"It's Denim!" she yelled back at him.

Denim giggled at the siblings' exchange. She remembered clearly how her brother Antoine would do the exact same thing with her when they were growing up. Since he had gone off to college she sorely missed times like these.

"I like your shoes," Tiffany complimented Denim on her purple and gold Nikes.

"Thank you, I got them at that new shoe store in the mall."

Levar ran down the stairs and found Denim dressed in a pair of tight-fitting jeans and a Langley High T-shirt.

"What brings you over here?" he asked as he led her into the family room.

"Well, I was in the area visiting a friend and I was going to the mall to get a manicure and pedicure. I thought I would check with your mom to see if it's okay if Tiffany went with me, my treat."

Levar was unsure if Tiffany would be up to doing anything like that after their earlier conversation. Besides, she didn't know Denim and thought Kyra would be better suited to spend some girl time with Tiffany but he found out she was grounded for smart-mouthing her mother, so finding Denim in his foyer was a God sent.

"Are you sure about this?" he asked curiously. "Tiffany don't take to strangers too quickly."

"Yes, I'm sure, but if she don't want to go I truly understand. Maybe we need more time to get to know each other before hanging out like this. I know what it's like having an older brother and being the only girl in the family. My parents worked too and my mother didn't always have time to hang out with me like I wanted her to. I had someone who took an interest in me when I was her age so I'm just returning the favor. I see a little of myself in Tiffany."

"I think it's great but my mom's still at work and I don't know if she'll go for it since she just met you recently."

"I understand," she admitted as she turned to open the door to leave,"but if you find out otherwise, let me know."

"I want to go," Tiffany revealed as she stepped inside the room. "I'm sure Momma will let me go if I talk to her."

Levar looked at Tiffany, who already had her purse on her shoulders. Hanging out with Denim might help get to the root of her behavior and what she was so afraid of, but Levar had his concerns. Tiffany was so upset earlier and he didn't want her to feel like he was pushing her off on Denim.

"Are you sure, Tiffany? You weren't feeling well a little while ago."

Tiffany pulled out her cell phone and said, "I'm sure." She immediately dialed her mother's work number. She really did want to go with Denim because she was different from Kyra. Denim was stylish and more girlie in her opinion. Kyra was pretty but into sports and was stuck under Levar all the time.

While Tiffany spoke to her mother, Levar and Denim talked about work. Seconds later, Tiffany held her cell phone out to Levar so he could talk to his mom. Once everything was confirmed, Levar walked Tiffany out to Denim's car and watched as they drove off down the street.

At the mall, Tiffany's mood seemed to improve after being pampered by the salon attendants. She decided to get the tips of her nails painted in her school colors and selected a toe ring for her freshly manicured toes.

"I like your nails, Tiffany. Those colors are pretty."

Tiffany held out her hand and admired her nails.

"Thank you, they're my school colors."

After paying the cashier, Denim looked at her watch and asked, "Do you feel like getting something to eat?"

"I guess," Tiffany replied softly.

"Good, because I'm starving. The food court is just around the corner. What do you have a taste for?"

Tiffany thought to herself and then said, "Well, I like Chinese and I like gyros, but to be honest, I don't know what I want."

"Let's walk through and look at everything before we decide. I'm up for whatever, but that pizza really smells good."

After walking past all the food vendors, Tiffany decided upon chicken tenders and fries and Denim selected a calzone. They chose a table and sat down to enjoy their meals. The two sat quietly together as they ate their food. Then out of nowhere Tiffany asked, "Do you have a boyfriend?"

Denim smiled quietly as she thought about Dré.

"Yes, I have a boyfriend. His name is Dré. Well, his name is André but I call him Dré."

Without making eye contact Tiffany asked, "How long have you been with him?"

Denim thought to herself for a few seconds and then said, "Well, that's hard to say. We grew up together and I've loved him for a long time so I guess you can say all my life."

Then out of nowhere Tiffany asked, "Have you ever let him touch you?"

Startled, Denim froze. She wasn't sure what was going on, but Tiffany was a young teen and obviously had questions; therefore, she responded carefully. "What do you mean, touch me?"

Somewhat embarrassed, Tiffany lowered her eyes and said, "You know . . ."

Denim put her fork down and reached across the table and tilted Tiffany's chin upward so she could look into her eyes. "What exactly are you asking me, Tiffany?"

Tiffany took a deep breath and asked, "Have you ever, you know, had sex with him?"

Denim smiled and then blushed, giving Tiffany her answer.

"You'll learn as you get older that it's not good to kiss and tell, but I can tell you that Dré and I love each other very much. He's the only guy for me and we plan to get married after we graduate from college," she announced. "Why did you ask me that anyway? Because it's really a personal question."

Tiffany took a long sip of her soda and said, "I

was just curious. You're really pretty and I figured you would tell me. In my opinion, I think it's gross."

"And just how would you know, young lady?" Denim joked after thanking her for the compliment.

Tiffany looked at her with tears in her eyes and lied. "I don't know, but I heard some of my friends talking about it."

"What's up with the tears? From being around you the short time I've know you and your family, you shouldn't be crying unless they're tears of joy," Denim explained.

"I'm sorry, I've been a little emotional lately," Tiffany replied.

"You're thirteen, right?" Denim asked.

Tiffany nodded in agreement.

"Is some boy putting pressure on you to do something you're not ready to do?" Denim asked.

Tiffany shook her head without verbally responding.

"Listen, Tiffany, I have a close friend who rushed life and now she's sitting at home with a baby. I don't want that to be me and I wouldn't want it for you either. Being intimate with a boy changes your life and while it can be a beautiful thing, it can also be the worse thing that ever happened to you. Do you understand where I'm coming from?"

She nodded in silence once again.

Denim let out a loud sigh. She felt like she was getting closer to finding out what was going on with Tiffany but she didn't want to risk her totally withdrawing. If she did that she'd probably never find out what was bothering her.

Tiffany dipped a chicken tender into her honey mustard and said, "Thank you."

Denim reached across the table and held Tiffany's hand.

"You're welcome. Making the right and safest choices is the best thing you can ever do for yourself. Rushing into something like boys is never good. You have to know for sure the boy is not lying to you and that he truly loves and respects you. So many guys trick girls into believing they love them when all they want is one thing and then they dump them right afterwards so they move on to the next girl."

At that moment Tiffany's suspicions came true. Denim had turned out to be a friend she could talk to. Someone who would listen and not judge her or make her feel like a child.

"Denim, can I tell you something?" she asked as she pulled her hand back and grabbed another chicken tender.

"Sure! You can ask or tell me anything."

Tiffany's heart was beating hard in her chest. She was still nervous about telling her secret because she didn't want her assailant to hurt her mother or Levar, but she couldn't continue to live in fear. She needed to tell someone and at the moment telling Denim felt right.

Denim took a bit of her calzone and waited as Tiffany tried to find the right words to say.

"Somebody touched me in a bad way," she blurted out.

Denim nearly choked as she looked across the table at Tiffany, whose eyes were once again filled with tears. She coughed a couple of times and then took a sip of her soda to clear her throat before speaking.

"Excuse me?" Denim asked angrily. "What do you mean, someone touched you?"

"Some guy molested me," Tiffany nervously revealed.

"Molested you? Oh my God. When did this happen?" Denim asked urgently.

Tiffany squirmed in her seat before answering. "It happened a few weeks ago."

Panic swept over Denim's body as Tiffany's words sank into her mind. She had to regain her composure and try to stay calm, but she was having a hard time doing so.

"Have the police arrested the guy?" Denim asked.

Tiffany lowered her head and said, "Nobody knows about it. You're the first person I've told."

Denim got her thoughts together before she spoke. She was angry that some pervert put his hands on such an innocent young girl and sad that she had to experience such a terrible ordeal.

"Why haven't you told your mother or Levar? They need to know about this so they can report it to the police," Denim frantically advised her. "Who did it? Was it someone at your school?"

"No." Tiffany replied. She felt like her head was spinning from all the questions Denim was throwing at her.

"Then who did it?" Denim asked as her voice got louder.

"I don't want to go to police, I just want to forget about it," Tiffany explained.

"You can't forget about something like this." Denim replied as she slammed her hand on the table.

"Yes, I can," Tiffany screamed back at her as she threw her napkin onto her food tray and stood.

Tiffany's head was starting to spin. Then the sound of her assailant's voice whispering in her ears came back to haunt her. He said he would kill her and her family if she ever told anyone. His threatening words had kept her quiet but now the secret was out and she panicked.

"Tiffany, you can't let him have this power over you," Denim urged her young friend. "You have to tell your mother. If you don't he will molest someone else, maybe someone even younger than you."

"I said forget it!" Tiffany urged Denim as she jumped out of her chair.

Denim also stood. She put her arm around Tiffany's shoulders and said, "I care about you, Tiffany. I can't forget something like this. You need to go to the police."

"I can't, Denim! He said he would kill me and my family if I ever told."

Denim tilted her chin and softly said, "That's how they get away with it, Tiffany. You can't let him control you like that. You have to tell."

Tiffany backed away from Denim and said, "I can't, Denim. I want to go home."

"We're not going anywhere until you agree to tell your mother and go to the police," Denim announced as she folded her arms in defiance and stared at Tiffany.

"I thought I could trust you. That's the only reason I told you," Tiffany explained.

"You can trust me, Tiffany. Let me help you put

this pervert behind bars," she pleaded. "Now please tell me who hurt you?"

Tiffany grabbed her tray off the table and walked over to a nearby trash bin without answering. She dumped the empty food containers into the trash bin and then turned back to Denim.

"Are you going to take me home or not?"

"Of course I'll take you home, but Tiffany, please listen to me," Denim pleaded with her once more. "You have to talk to your mother."

Tiffany took Denim by the hand and led her over to a more private area of the food court. There she told her how and where the man touched her. Once she was finished telling Denim all the disgusting details she burst into tears.

"I don't even know who did it, Denim. I didn't see his face or recognize his voice because he whispered the whole time so please just take me home."

Denim hugged Tiffany and said, "It's going to be all right, Tiffany. I'm going to help you."

"Please don't tell anyone, especially Levar. I don't want him to get into any trouble."

Denim thought about the anxiety Tiffany must be going though. Here she was, barely a teenager and had been through one of the worse things imaginable. She wasn't exactly sure what she was going to do to help Tiffany but she knew she had to do something and fast.

Regina got in from work, showered, and started preparing dinner. Levar walked into the kitchen and asked, "Why is Dexter having his friends meet him here?"

"Are you talking about Paul?" she asked as she stirred the mushroom-flavored rice.

"Yes, Ma'am"

"Oh, Paul's okay, son."

"That's not the point, Momma. Dexter doesn't run things here. I'm still the man of the house."

She put the spoon down and leaned against the counter.

"You're right, Levar, and I apologize that no one told you about Paul coming by to meet Dexter. He actually thought that he was going to get here before Paul but he got delayed at the last minute."

"So you knew he was coming?" Levar asked his mother.

She put her hands in the air as a sign of surrender.

"Yes, I knew he was coming over, but like I said, we didn't expect Paul to get here first. Sweetheart,

I got called into a meeting before I could call you. I'm sorry."

Levar stared at his mother in disbelief.

"Listen Momma, I know you're busy at work and all in love with Dexter but you can't forget to tell me stuff like that. I didn't like the way he walked in my yard like he was supposed to be here."

Regina hugged her son's neck and said, "I'm so glad that you're protective of our home, but you're going to have to understand that once I'm married to Dexter his friends and family will be coming over."

Levar picked up a buttered roll sitting on a serving tray and asked, "But until then, I'm still in charge when you're not here and while we're on the subject, once you marry Dexter, what does that mean for us?"

She pulled a casserole tray of lemon pepper chicken out of the oven and asked, "What are you talking about?"

"Are we going to have to move in with Dexter or is Dexter moving in here?"

"That's something we've been discussing but we haven't come to a decision yet," she revealed as she removed her oven mittens.

"The last thing Dexter wants to do is uproot you

guys from your home. There are so many memo-
ries here and we both know it keeps you guys tied
to your father. Wherever we end up, Levar, remember that your father will always be a part of our
lives. I see him in both you and Tiffany and no matter what, I'll always love him. There's no way I
could ever forget him or the life we had together."

"I'm cool with wherever we go as long as we
don't have to change schools and it's not too far
from Kyra, my job, and our grandparents."

Regina hugged Levar and said, "I agree and we
wouldn't have it any other way."

About that time, Tiffany and Denim entered the
house. Tiffany immediately ran up the stairs before
Regina and Levar could see her.

Levar walked into the foyer and asked, "Where's
Tiffany?"

Lying, Denim said, "She's upstairs. She had to go
to the bathroom."

What she didn't know how to tell him was that
his sister had told her a terrible secret and had ar-
gued about it before returning.

"So, did you ladies have a good time getting
pampered?" he asked as he led her into the dining
room.

Forcing a smile, she said, "Yes, we had a nice

time together. I hope to get to spend more time with her."

Regina smiled when Denim entered the kitchen. "Hello, Denim."

"Hi, Mrs. Ray."

She sat a bowl of green beans on the table and said, "That was really sweet of you to treat Tiffany to the manicure. I stay so busy that I don't have as much time to spend with her as I would like."

Denim waved her off and said, "It was okay. I enjoyed her company."

"Is it okay if Denim stays for dinner?" Levar asked.

"Where are my manners? Of course she can."

"Oh, no, Mrs. Ray, I really have to get going. Maybe another time," Denim replied.

"Are you sure? We'd love for you to stay and I'm sure Tiffany would too."

"Thank you, but I really have to go. I'm going to go say good-bye to Tiffany on my way out. Have a great evening and it was nice seeing you again, Mrs. Ray."

"Likewise, Denim."

Denim gave Levar a hug and said, "Good-bye, Levar. I'll see you at work tomorrow."

* * *

Upstairs Denim found Tiffany on her computer. Even though her door was opened she still knocked before entering.

"May I come in?"

Without looking in her direction Tiffany answered, "If you want to."

Denim slowly walked over to her and sat down in a nearby chair.

"I'm getting ready to go but I wanted to come up to tell you I'm sorry I yelled at you."

"It's cool," Tiffany replied. "I'm sorry I yelled at you too."

"Tiffany?" Denim called out to her. "Could you turn around and talk to me for a second?"

She let out a loud breath and turned around to face Denim.

"I know today was our first day hanging out, but I want you to know that I care about you. I also want you to know that I understand why you're afraid to tell your mom and Levar. What you experienced was terrible, but you really need to think hard about telling them about what happened to you. They love you and only want to keep you safe."

Tiffany pointed her finger at Denim and said, "I'm not telling them and neither are you."

Denim stood and pulled her purse on her shoulders in defeat. She had hoped to talk Tiffany into confiding in someone in an authority position, but she was unsuccessful.

"I really wish you would reconsider," she said as she turned to walk out of her room. "By the way, your mom has your dinner ready so you'd better get downstairs before they get suspicious. I told them you had to go to the bathroom."

Before Denim could get out into the hallway, Tiffany ran over and hugged her waist, stopping her in her tracks. Denim put her arms around her shoulders and embraced her as well, putting a smile on her face.

"Thanks for letting me hang out with you today, Denim. I really did have fun."

"It was my pleasure," Denim replied. "We'll do it again real soon."

Tiffany released her and said, "I'd like that."

With her arm around Tiffany's shoulder, she said, "Come on so you can walk me to the door."

Tiffany walked her downstairs and out to her car before slowly making her way back into the house.

Chapter Ten

Denim felt like she was driving in a daze. The situation with Tiffany had affected her personally and she couldn't sit by and watch her deteriorate emotionally or stay quiet. There was a monster on the streets and it was only a matter of time before he struck again. Needing some comforting, she took a chance and drove to the park in hopes of finding Dré. He often played basketball there with several friends when he wasn't painting or at basketball practice. When she pulled into the parking space near the basketball courts she found Dré, his friend DeMario, and a few other guys playing a pickup game of basketball. It was an unseasonably warm day and he looked so handsome in his navy and white shorts and matching Nike T-shirt. Basketball was his passion, along with painting.

As she sat and watched him play like so many times before, she appreciated just how gifted and sexy he was. She turned off the ignition and pulled her diary out of her purse.

Dear Diary,
*   Today wasn't a good day. I spent the day with the sister of good friend and found out she was hiding a horrible secret, a secret that has changed her life and has her living in fear. I'm trying my best to help her but she's afraid. I'm praying for guidance and that my friend reaches out to me, her mother or someone close to her real soon.*
Later
D

She tucked her diary back into her purse and then climbed out of the car.

"Dré, here comes your girl," one of his friends announced.

Dré smiled as he watched her walk toward him in her body-hugging jeans and so did the rest of the guys on the court. One of them took things a little too far when he pointed at Denim and said, "Dré, watch your back because if you mess up with that, I'm going to be all over her."

Dré turned and gave his friend an unwelcome glare and said, "Don't make me hurt you, bro."

All the guys burst into laughter as they replenished their bodies with Gatorade and water while Dre` turned his attention back to Denim.

"Mercy," he mumbled under his breath as he admired her natural beauty. He met her halfway to the basketball court where she immediately hugged him tightly around the neck. Dré returned the hug and instantly knew something was wrong.

"Dang, babe. What's up?" he asked as he gently caressed her back.

She smiled and said, "I just needed one of your hugs."

He gazed into her eyes and said, "Are you okay? You look like something's bothering you."

DeMario yelled over to him.

"Come on Dré, are you going to play ball or are you going to snuggle with Denim all day."

Denim could hear the guys on the basketball court laughing at DeMario's remark. She backed away and said, "I didn't mean to interrupt your game."

Ignoring DeMario and his friends, Dré grabbed her hand to prevent her from leaving.

"Forget them. You know I'll stop anything for you. You're all I care about. Now tell me what's wrong. I can see you're almost in tears."

She caressed his cheeks before kissing him softly on the lips.

"Go finish playing with your friends. I'll call you later."

"Are you sure?" he asked as he walked her to the car and opened the door for her.

Denim wasn't sure whether she should tell Dré about Tiffany or not. She needed to talk to someone, but she needed to get her emotions in check first.

"I'll be okay, baby. I'm just having a moment," she replied as she turned the key and revved up her Mustang's engine. "And tell DeMario I don't have time for him right now but I'll kick his butt later."

Dré laughed at her comment. DeMario was not only his best friend but friends with Denim as well.

"I love you," she whispered softly.

"I love you too," he responded as he gave her one more kiss. "Drive carefully."

She smiled as she backed out of the parking space and pulled off while Dré hurried back to the basketball court to finish his game.

Tiffany opened her closet and saw the trash bag filled with the clothes she was wearing the night of her attack. Immediately the images of that horrible night came flooding back to her. She closed her eyes and tried to stifle the nauseating feeling in her stomach. She just wished she had seen his face, and then maybe she would be able to sleep in peace. Not knowing was driving her crazy.

"Tiffany, are you okay?" Dexter asked as he stepped into her room.

Startled, she jumped and slammed her closet door closed.

"Don't you knock?" she asked angrily as she moved away from the closet.

"Sweetheart, I knocked and called your name several times," he explained as he glanced over at her closet and walked further in the room.

"What do you want?" Tiffany asked as she sat down at her computer.

"I came to find out what happened with the double Dutch competition. Your mother told me you quit the team."

"I'm not feeling it anymore. It's no big deal."

"I think it is a big deal," Dexter replied as he folded his arms. "You were excited about it a few weeks ago and I think you have a great chance of winning this year."

"Well it's not going to happen because I'm not jumping."

Dexter scratched his head in disbelief but he decided not to question her anymore.

"Well, goodnight. If you need anything or just want to talk, I want you to know I'm a good listener."

She nodded as she grabbed her cell phone and pretended to text someone. Dexter turned and walked out of her room, closing the door behind him. Tiffany took the bag of clothes out of her closet and stuffed them in her book bag so she could throw them in a Dumpster at school tomorrow.

Denim was quiet through dinner and she continued to worry about Tiffany. Afterward she sat in the family room and watched TV with her dad. He looked over at her and pointed out the fact that she'd been quiet all evening.

"I'm fine, Daddy."

Just then her cell phone rang. "Hello?"

"What are you doing?" Dré asked.

"I'm watching TV with Daddy."

"Ask him if I can come over."

"Daddy, Dré wants to know if he can come over."

Samuel looked at his watch and said, "Yeah, but only for a little while."

"He said yes," Denim announced as she got up and walked out of the room.

"Good, because I'm already outside."

Denim and Dré spent the next hour talking about their future. It was almost dark as they sat out on her porch talking about college and marriage. Denim seemed to be in another world as she sat next to the love of her life, hugging her knees.

"Are you listening to me or am I talking to myself?" he asked.

"Huh?" she replied as she snapped back to reality.

"Where were you? Because you weren't here with me."

Denim wanted to confide in Dré about Tiffany but it was a delicate matter and she didn't know if she should involve him. What she did know was that someone in Tiffany's family needed to know about the assault. For all she knew it could be a family member. Time was of the essence and Denim knew she would have to do something and fast.

"I'm sorry, Dré, I'm listening, I just have a lot on my mind," she apologized as she linked her arm with his and laid her head on his shoulder. "I can't wait to graduate from college and marry you too."

He leaned over and kissed her slowly on the lips

and said, "I was just checking. You were so quiet I wasn't sure if you'd changed your mind."

She nuzzled her face against his warm neck and said, "Never."

"I'd better go before you Dad comes out here and runs me out of the yard."

Denim cupped his face and said, "Momma and Daddy love you, Dré."

"Not if they knew what I was doing to you."

She blushed.

"Well, they were young once. Besides, I've already told them that you're the only one for me."

He stepped down off the steps and said, "But you're their baby and no parent wants to think of their baby in that way."

"I may be *their* baby but they have to realize that I'm not a baby anymore. In another year I'll be eighteen," she replied as she stood and dusted off the back of her jeans, causing Dré's eyes to immediately go to her backside. Denim caught him staring at her and gave him a tender nudge. She loved it when he admired her body and loved it even more when she was in his arms.

"Go home, Prime Time, because you're making my heart beat faster."

He backed away from her and said, "I don't have

to tell you what you're doing to me. You're danger-ous, Cocoa Princess."

"Baby, you don't have a thing to worry about because all of this is for you and you only," she announced as she twirled around to give him a complete view of her heavenly body.

Pleased upon hearing her commitment to him, he said, "Now that's what I'm talking about. Later, baby," he answered as he quickly climbed into his car and pulled out of her driveway.

A couple more weekends quickly came and went as well as weeks of school and work. Levar still couldn't put his finger on Tiffany's behavior, which seemed to be getting worse. Since Kyra was still on punishment, he continued to support Denim and Tiffany's newfound friendship. He was prayer-ful that Denim could get to the bottom of his sister's personality change and losts of interest in every-thing she once loved, especially jumping rope.

Over the past few weekends Denim spent time with Tiffany and worked on convincing her to talk to her mother about the assault. It weighed heavily on Denim's heart and looking Levar in the face at work everyday wasn't easy. What Tiffany had expe-rienced had changed her life forever and she needed help, both physically and emotionally.

"So Denim, have you found out why Tiffany's tripping?" he asked as he helped her straighten up the physical therapy room.

She lied without making eye contact with him.

"Not really. Tiffany's a teenager now and we girls go through a lot. She's growing up, Levar."

"I know she's growing up, but to suddenly stop jumping rope is just strange."

Denim tossed a couple of Pilates balls over to him and said, "Maybe she thinks it's too childish since she'll be in high school next year. How long has she been jumping rope?"

"Since she was six years old," he revealed. "It's all she's ever loved."

Denim helped Levar put the hand weights back on their rack.

"I'm sure there are a few things you've outgrown over the years," Denim suggested.

"Not really. I've played football, basketball, and baseball. I like trying different things."

"She's a girl, Levar. We're not wired like you guys," she pointed out. "Tiffany is probably going through the stage of trying to figure out what she wants to do next. Maybe she felt pressured by the double Dutch competition."

"I hope you're right because I don't know how much more of her attitude I can take. She used to be so happy. Now she acts like she's angry all the time and she spends all her time in her room. She's even lost interest in hanging with her friends," he revealed as he handed Denim her jacket and then slid into his own.

Denim had taken all she could take. Hearing Levar's sincere concern for his sister had gotten the best of her and she cracked.

"Levar, I have something to tell you but you have to promise you won't go crazy on me."

He looked up at her and asked, "Go crazy? It must be bad if you say that. What is it?"

"It's about Tiffany. Something happened to her. I was trying to give her time to tell you or your mother but she's taking too long and you guys need to know."

Fear swept over Levar as he braced himself for whatever Denim was about to tell him. He sat down on a nearby stool and with his voice cracking, he asked, "What happened to her?"

Denim pulled another stool over to Levar and held both his hands. She closed her eyes and then told him as gently as she could, "Tiffany's been hurt by someone."

"What do you mean, hurt?"

"She was molested, Levar."

He jumped up, nearly knocking Denim to the

floor and yelled, "What the hell are you talking about? Tiffany would tell me if something like that happened to her."

"Would she, Levar? Think about what she's been through and how traumatic it was."

"Are you serious?" he yelled.

Levar felt dizzy and nauseated. His head was pounding and he was ready to kill.

"I'm sorry to have to tell you, Levar, but Tiffany tried to make me promise not to tell anyone because whoever did it threatened to kill her and your whole family."

Levar's face had changed colors and it appeared that steam was rising out of his jacket.

"Who did it?"

"You have to stay calm, Levar."

"Stay calm!" he yelled. "How the hell can I stay calm with information like this?"

"You have to stay calm because that's all I know. I don't know when it happened and she told me she didn't see his face, so she doesn't even know who did it."

Levar put his hands over his face and paced the floor. "Why didn't you tell me sooner?"

"I wanted to, but I was trying to get more information out of her. She clams up every time I push her for more information."

"Was it Dexter?" he asked.

"Dexter? You mean your future stepfather?"

"Hell, yeah!" he yelled. "He seems to want to hang around Tiffany more than I'm comfortable with."

"Levar, think about it. Tiffany would know if it was Dexter. I believe her when she said she doesn't know the person."

"I have to get out of here," he replied as he made a break for the door.

Denim grabbed his arm, stopping him. She was afraid that he would run home and yell at Tiffany, causing her to withdraw even further. If she did that they might never find out who assaulted her.

"Wait a second. What are you going to do?" she asked.

Tears welled up in Levar's eyes. "I'm going home to talk to my sister because I've broken my promise to her."

"What promise?" Denim asked.

"I promised Tiffany I would never let anything happen to her."

"Broken promises?" she asked. "Levar, this has nothing to do with that. It's not your fault. Tiffany needs your to help. She's scared, she's hurt, and she's ashamed. Be her brother, not a vigilante."

Levar hugged Denim and said, "It's not that easy.

When I get my hands on the person who did this, he's dead."

"Levar you can't . . ." she replied.

"No, Denim. Don't try to talk me out of it," he yelled. "I'm going to handle this."

She released him and then pointed her finger at him. "Levar, please don't do anything that could ruin your life."

He pulled his car keys out of his pocket and said, "I can't promise you that. I'll call you later."

Denim walked him to the door, feeling defeated. She had set in motion a change of events that could affect the life of Levar's entire family. She closed her eyes and prayed that Levar kept a level head so he could help his sister.

When Levar burst through the door, of his house, he found it empty. As he made his way into the kitchen he spotted a note on the refrigerator from his mother. As he read the note, he found out that Dexter was hosting a poker game and that his mom and Tiffany were on their way to his house to drop off some food. Still not convinced that Dexter wasn't the person who assaulted his sister, he ran upstairs into his mother's bedroom and grabbed his father's .38 caliber handgun out of her closet and headed out the door.

Chapter Eleven

As Tiffany helped her mother carry the food and drinks into Dexter's kitchen they could hear the sound of familiar laughter coming from his family room. Seconds later, Dexter joined them and immediately picked up a chicken tender and took a bite.

"Thanks for picking the food up for me, babe," he said before giving her a kiss. "I just got home about thirty minutes ago. Everyone else should be here shortly."

"I didn't mind, sweetheart," she replied as she wiped her lipstick off his lips.

Dexter then turned to Tiffany and smiled.

"So how are you doing today, young lady?"

Before she could answer, Paul walked into the kitchen.

"Okay, Dexter, I have the poker table set up and

the beer is on ice. Oh, something smells delicious. Is that chicken wings I smell?"

He gave Regina a hug and said, "Hello, Regina. I didn't know you were here."

She smiled and said, "Hello, Paul. We just stopped by to drop off food and drinks for you guys and to answer your question, no, I brought chicken tenders, not chicken wings."

He clapped his hands together and then rubbed his stomach.

"You can't go wrong with the bird," he answered.

Regina pulled the cellophane off the other platters and said, "You also have fried cheese sticks and a few other things goodies I'm sure you guys are going to enjoy."

Paul then turned to Tiffany, gently patted her on the back and said, "You're looking very pretty today too, my sweet angel."

Tiffany looked up at Paul and then took a step back. Dexter noticed that her body had tensed up and she began to tremble.

"What's wrong, Tiffany?" Dexter inquired as he watched Tiffany's demeanor change.

Ignoring his question, she walked over to her mother and gently took her by the arm.

"I'm ready to go home, Momma."

Regina didn't understand why Tiffany was suddenly clinging to her but things went from strange to bizarre when Levar burst into the kitchen and pointed the gun directly at Dexter.

"Levar!" Regina screamed. "What are doing with that gun?"

Dexter put his hands up in surrender as he looked down the barrel of the gun.

"I'm going to kill you for what you did to my sister!" he yelled.

"What the hell are you talking about? I didn't do anything to Tiffany," Dexter defensively explained.

Paul didn't know what to do, run or try to make a move on Levar. Regina continued to scream at her son, pleading with him to put the gun down before someone got killed. The whole scene was chaotic and surreal and Levar didn't show any signs of relinquishing his stance.

"Momma, how could you marry this monster? He hurt Tiffany!"

Regina looked into the gentle face of her fiancée and then back at her son.

"Dexter would never hurt Tiffany. You're not making any sense."

"He molested her, Momma, and now he's going to pay for all her pain!"

Regina's eyes quickly filled with tears. There was no way it could be true. How could the man she loved do such a horrific thing to her daughter, her baby? But this was her son and he wouldn't lie to her about something so sick, disgusting, and evil.

"Is it true?" she asked as the tears spilled out of her eyes. "Did you hurt my baby?"

In somewhat of a traumatized state, Tiffany continued to tug on her mother's arm without taking her eyes off Paul.

"I want to go home," she pleaded.

"Did you hurt my child?" Regina screamed at Dexter.

"Wait just a damn minute! I didn't do anything to Tiffany. Sweetheart, tell them!" Dexter pleaded.

Regina sobbed as she watched her son's finger began to squeeze the trigger on the gun. Then just before he pulled the trigger, Tiffany screamed out, "Dexter didn't hurt me, it was him!"

All eyes went to Paul as Tiffany pointed at Dexter's longtime friend.

"Hold up," he said as he backed away from Levar.

Dexter looked into the eyes of his best friend and saw something he'd seen before: guilt. Then without hesitating, he punched him dead in the face, knocking him over the table and onto the floor.

"You son of a bitch!" he yelled as he grabbed the

gun out of Levar's hand and pointed it at Paul's head. "Did you put your hands on this child?"

"Hold up, bro. You know me!" Paul yelled.

Dexter looked over at Tiffany and asked, "Is he the one who hurt you, sweetheart?"

Tiffany nodded with tears streaming down her face.

"This is real important, Tiffany. Are you sure— and I mean are you without a doubt in your mind— sure it was Paul?" he asked as he held the gun steady to try and confirm her answer.

"Yes, Dexter, I'm sure. He said he would kill me and Levar and then slit Momma's throat if I ever told anybody what he did to me."

"Get the kids out of here, Regina!" Dexter yelled frantically. "They don't need to be here."

"I'm sorry, baby," she apologized to him.

"It's okay, just get the kids and get out," he yelled again.

"What are you going to do?" she asked as she reached for her purse and car keys.

"Just go, Regina," he replied. "I got this."

"Dexter, I'm sorry about pointing the gun at you," Levar apologized. He felt bad that he nearly killed Dexter over his suspicions and not the facts.

"It's okay, son. I would've done the same thing you did. Now go home with your mother."

Levar stood next to Dexter and said, "No, I'm not going anywhere. I want to stay here with you."

"You did your part, son. Now it's time for me do mine. Now go on home with your mother," Dexter calmly instructed Levar. "I'll see you later."

Regina quickly pushed Tiffany and Levar out the door, leaving Dexter alone with Paul. Once he was sure they were gone, Dexter immediately pulled the trigger, shooting Paul in the knee. Paul screamed out in excruciating pain.

"You sick bastard! I should blow your ass away right now for what you did to that child. What the hell is wrong with you?"

With sweat dripping down his face, Paul said, "Go right ahead, but you'll be the one sitting in jail for the rest of your life, not me."

Dexter thought about what Paul said. He was, after all, a lawyer and he knew the court system inside and out, so the chances he would get off for the crime was very high, especially since the victim was a minor. Dexter was beside himself and he had to gather his thoughts quickly in order to deal with his former friend. The blood from Paul's leg wound was seeping through his pants leg and was starting to drip onto the floor. He needed to hear the facts from Paul's mouth before doing anything else.

Dexter pushed the cold steel barrel against Paul's other knee and said, "Tell me what you did to Tiffany before I blow you away."

Paul's breathing was rapid and he moaned in pain as he contemplated his response.

"Answer me!" Dexter yelled, causing Paul to flinch.

"I couldn't help myself. My doctor said—"

"Doctor?" Dexter asked. "What kind of doctor?"

"I'm in therapy, bro. I'm being treated for it," Paul admitted.

"I'm not going to let you hide behind some high-priced shrink. You're a pervert and if I decide to let you live you're going to tell the police what you did. If you don't, you don't want to know what I'm going to do to you," Dexter lectured him. "Do you understand?"

"I'm not going to throw away my career over that girl. So what if I touched her a little bit. It's my word against hers."

"Wrong answer!" Dexter yelled before pulling the trigger. As Paul screamed, he thought of the pain Tiffany went through and how scared she must've been, making it easier to accept what he'd done. His plans were to spend the rest of his life with Regina and the kids but if he didn't protect them, what did that say about him as a potential husband and father? He just hoped that they would eventually forgive him for bringing Paul into their lives.

"Are you going to let me bleed to death?" Paul screamed out. "Call the paramedics!"

Dexter sat in the kitchen chair and calmly asked, "Does it hurt?"

"Hell yeah, it hurts! I'm sorry, okay?"

Paul moaned and groaned in pain. He realized that Dexter wasn't going to call for help until he confessed his crime so he did just that until Dexter was satisfied and only then did he call paramedics and police and turned himself in.

At the Ray house, Regina sat up in her bed and held a sleeping Tiffany in her arms. Two hours had passed since they had left Dexter's house and he still hadn't called. Not knowing where he was or what he'd done had her nerves frayed. As she looked down at her daughter's angelic face and stroked her hair, it made her heart ache. She still wasn't sure what Paul had done to her but she knew it had altered their lives forever. Now she understood why Tiffany had quit jumping rope and pushed away from her friends. The signs were there, she was just too caught up in work and her upcoming wedding to see it.

Making sure Tiffany received counseling and making Paul pay for what he'd done was a priority in making sure that Tiffany got past the trauma so she could get back to being a teenager and to doing the things she loved.

Levar sat out on the front porch steps in the cool night air and nervously waited for Dexter to arrive. As he waited he wondered if life for his family would ever be happy again. He couldn't take much more. First they experienced the tragic death of his father and now this. It was too much and for the first time in a long time, he allowed himself to cry. He felt helpless and while he knew it wasn't considered manly to cry, this was different. Just then he received a text message from Kyra. He already had several missed calls and messages from her but he had yet to answer any of them. He knew he needed to call or text her before she showed up so he sent her a text until he was emotionally able to talk to her.

Kyra,
I'm fine. Sorry I haven't called. I got a lot going on at home right now. I'll call you tomorrow.
Luv You,
Levar

Just as he pushed the send button on his cell phone he noticed headlights pulling into the driveway. He wiped his tear-streaked face and tried to regain his composure. That's when he realized that the car wasn't Dexter's, but Denim's. He met her at the car and asked, "What are you doing here?"

She opened the car door and stepped out until she was face-to-face with him.

"I haven't heard back from you. I wanted to make sure you were okay. How's Tiffany?"

He put his hands over his face and said, "Tiffany will be fine. Look, Denim, I appreciate you coming by but this is really not a good time."

"You don't look so good."

"I can't talk about it right now. You should go home and I'll tell you later."

Denim touched his arm to soothe her dear friend.

"I can tell you're upset. You didn't do anything stupid, did you?"

He opened her car door for her and said, "No, but I came real close to it. It's hard dealing with what happened, you know?"

Denim looked into his eyes. She could clearly see that he was dealing with the situation as best he could. She just prayed that he hadn't done anything crazy and that Tiffany was on the road to recovery.

Denim climbed back inside her car and said, "You and your family will get through this, Levar. Just take one day at a time. Okay?"

He closed her car door and said, "I will. Drive carefully and thanks for coming by."

She put the car in reverse and said, "You're welcome and call me if you want to talk."

He nodded and then watched as she backed out of his driveway and down the street.

Levar returned to the front steps and sat down. He reached into his pocket, pulled out his cell phone, and pulled up Dexter's phone number and stared at it. The waiting was driving him crazy, making the urge to call him even stronger. But what if he didn't answer, then what? He had to know that he was okay and that Paul was on his way to the morgue. It was at that moment that he pushed the button and called the number. As it rang on the other end he nervously shook his leg. There was no answer and then the house telephone rang. He quickly ran into the house and grabbed the telephone. He immediately heard Dexter's voice talking to his mother, who had picked up on another extension. Before he could get a word out, Regina was already coming down the stairs and into the room. Levar hung up the phone and listened as his mother spoke to Dexter. He could see the agony in her face and hear the stress in her voice.

"What do you need me to do?" she asked Dexter.

Regina walked over to Levar and touched his face lovingly before sitting down on the sofa.

"What's going on?" Levar whispered to his mother.

She put her finger up as a signal for him to wait.

"Are you sure?" she asked Dexter as tears formed in her eyes and then she answered, "Okay, if you say so. I'll see you soon. I love you."

Regina hung up the telephone and covered her face with her hands.

"Dexter's been arrested. He shot Paul but he didn't kill him. He told us to wait here and not to talk to anyone until his attorney calls."

"They arrested Dexter and not Paul?" Levar asked. "I was hoping that he was dead."

She stood and said, "I understand how you feel, son. I'm sure Dexter knows what he's doing and I'm sure Paul will get arrested as soon as he's well enough to leave the hospital."

Levar paced the floor in disbelief. He wished Dexter had let Paul bleed to death. A slow, painful death was what he deserved.

"How can you be so sure Paul will get arrested? The man's a lawyer. He knows how to twist the truth around in his favor. I should've killed him when I had the chance."

Regina grabbed her son and pulled him into her arms and said, "You and I both know you wouldn't be able to live with that kind of burden on your heart."

He looked into his mother's eyes and said, "I have no problem living with killing the man who hurt my sister."

Before she replied he pulled away from her and ran up the stairs to his room.

At the police station Dexter was booked and put into a holding cell, where he would wait for his attorney to get him out. Detectives weren't able to question him, since he had invoked his right to counsel, leaving them puzzled as to the motive behind the shooting of his former best friend. If he didn't learn anything growing up in his rough neighborhood as a teenager, he learned first to never get into trouble—but if you did get into trouble to always ask for a lawyer. Now he would wait to be released so he could get back to the people he loved.

*   *   *

Denim sat on the side of her bed and thought about Tiffany and Levar and what they were going through as a family. It was all mind-numbing and hard to decipher, so she pulled out her diary and begin to write as she turned on the TV.

Dear Diary,
*   My friend Levar and his family are deal-*
ing with some serious drama right now.
Maybe more than I know. I just hope I did
the right thing by telling Levar about his sis-
ter. As far as I know her assailant is still un-
known and I'm sure she scared. I just pray
he's caught soon so Tiffany can get back to
being a teenager.
Later,
D

The next morning, Denim woke up to a news report of a shooting involving a prominent businessman. She wasn't paying close attention until she heard the familiar name, Dexter Banks.

"Where do I know that name from?" she asked herself as she slipped into her shoes.

Then his picture was shown on the screen and it

all came together. She pointed at the TV and said, "Oh my God! That's Levar's stepfather!"

She wasn't clear on what happened but had a sinking feeling that it may have had something to do with what happened to Tiffany. She grabbed her book bag and hurried downstairs. She would try to call Levar on the way to school.

Chapter Twelve

Paul lay in his hospital bed in a drug-induced daze. He had lost track of time but he hadn't forgotten who had put him there. He also hadn't forgotten why he was shot. As he laid there he looked down at his legs and observed the heavy bandaging. Dexter had done a number on him and he hoped he wasn't crippled for life. The sounds of the pulse and blood-pressure monitors beeped simultaneously as they kept track of his vital signs. It was a hypnotic sound, but he was startled when a baritone voice called out his name.

"Mr. Lindsey. I'm Detective Johns. I've been waiting for you to wake up so you could answer a few questions about the shooting. Are you up to it?"

Paul's eyes fluttered as he answered, "I'll try."

The detective took out his notepad and said,

"Well, it gets too much for you I can pick it up at another time."

Paul nodded and the detective began to ask about his relationship with Dexter. After explaining that he and Dexter were longtime friends, the detective then moved on to question him about the motive for the shooting. Paul struggled to reach the remote to raise his bed. Once he had the bed in a comfortable position, he thought about his last conversation with Dexter and the fact that he had confessed to touching the young girl, but he felt safe behind his doctor-patient confidentiality clause.

"Where is Dexter?" Paul asked the detective.

"Mr. Banks was booked and then released on bond. He'll have to appear in court in a few weeks but before that happens we need to get a statement from you on what happened. We already have Mr. Banks's statement."

Paul thought for a moment. If Dexter had been booked, there was a strong possibility that he didn't reveal anything about the girl. He was engaged to Regina and had grown quite fond of the kids and would spare Tiffany from an embarrassing trial if at all possible.

"What did he say?" Paul asked.

"I'm not at liberty to discuss Mr. Banks's statement, Mr. Lindsey. All we want is the truth so justice can be served."

"I understand, but I'm not feeling well. I think I'd rather wait until I'm out of the hospital before I answer any questions."

The detective put his notepad back in his pocket and said, "The longer we wait, the longer it'll take to resolve this matter."

Before walking out of the room, he put his business card on the table beside the bed and said, "Give me a call if you feel up to talking."

"I will," Paul replied as his eyes followed the detective as he made his way out the door.

The wheels in his mind were turning as he lay there. He needed to talk to his doctors as soon as possible. He needed to find out the extent of his injuries and how long he would be in the hospital, because it was going to be hard for him to defend himself unless he was released.

At Regina's house, Dexter sat next to Tiffany in the family room and held her hand lovingly. He was afraid that she would be a little reluctant to let him get close to her, but she did and it warmed his heart. Regina and Levar looked on as he assured her that he would do everything within his power to make sure that neither Paul nor any other man would ever hurt her again.

"Is he in jail?" Tiffany asked.

"Not yet," he replied. "But first I have to know if you are willing to tell the police what he did to you."

She gave his hand a squeeze and asked, "Where is he?"

Dexter hesitated answering. He looked at Regina and she nodded, signaling to him that it was okay to tell her.

"He's in the hospital right now and he'll probably be there for a while."

"You shot him, didn't you?" Tiffany asked with coldness in her voice.

He kissed her forehead and said, "Yes, I did, Tiffany. I shot him because he hurt you. I know it was wrong to take the law into my own hands, but I was angry. I feel like you guys are my family and nobody hurts my family."

"I wish you had let me shoot him," Levar said as he sat across the room.

"Why? So you could ruin your life?" Dexter yelled at Levar.

Levar jumped out of his chair and screamed, "He put his hands on my sister!"

Dexter stood and grabbed Levar by his shoulders to try and calm him.

"I wasn't going to let you make that kind of decision. Jail is not a place for you," Dexter informed him. "Besides, what would that do to your mother and your sister?"

He sank back down in his chair in silence. Tiffany walked over to him and put her arms around his neck and said, "I wouldn't want you to go to jail, Levar. I need to see you in the bleachers at my jump rope competitions."

With tears streaming down his face, Levar hugged her lovingly and said, "I wouldn't miss it for the world, Tiff."

Regina was also teary-eyed when she hugged Dexter. He kissed her on her soft lips and said, "We have a long road ahead of us. Tiffany needs counseling. I won't rest until that SOB Paul is in jail and I have to resolve the charges against me. Then after that—"

Interrupting him, Regina said, "And we still have a wedding to finalize."

"Do you think that's wise under the circumstances?" he asked as he nodded in the direction of the children.

Regina walked over to Tiffany and Levar and said, "Why don't we let them decide?"

"Decide what, Momma?" Tiffany asked.

Regina knelt in front of her children and softly

said, "I know we've just experienced some terrible, terrible things, but I want you guys to know that I love you more than life itself."

"We love you too, Momma," Tiffany replied.

She caressed their faces and said, "You guys also know how much I love Dexter and it should be obvious how much he loves you too. What I'm asking you guys is in spite of all the drama we just went through, are you up for a wedding? It doesn't have to be anything fancy. We can do it right here, just us and your grandparents. What do you say?"

Levar looked at Tiffany for some type of confirmation. He realized they needed to get through the horror Tiffany had experience and maybe the wedding was just what they needed to get things rolling.

"What do you think, Tiff?" Levar asked his sister.

"I think it would be cool. I like having Dexter around," she admitted as all four of them stood in the middle of the room and shared in a loving group hug.

The next afternoon, Tiffany and Levar, along with their grandparents, witnessed their mother and Dexter recite their vows by the fireplace in their family room. Afterward they all went out to dinner to celebrate. Their grandparents spent the night with them while Regina and Dexter honeymooned at his house. They had decided they would take a real honeymoon later. It was also decided that they would start fresh in a new house as soon as possible so Tiffany wouldn't have to relive her assault every time she entered the bathroom. It was going to be a welcoming move, which would still allow the kids to stay within their school zone with all their friends.

It didn't take Dexter and Regina long to find the perfect house to start their new lives. When Levar and Tiffany saw it they instantly fell in love with it and couldn't wait to move. Within a month of finding the house, they happily moved into their new home.

Once settled into their new home, Regina and Dexter met with Tiffany's counselor and then a lawyer to decide if they could be successful in prosecuting Paul for the assault. While the counselor felt like Tiffany was strong enough to handle a trial, their attorney told them without her clothes to test for DNA there wasn't enough evidence for an arrest for attempted rape. Instead, they had a shot at charging him molestation and even that wasn't promising, because there had never been any complaints against him and his medical records were sealed. Heartbroken, they had to break the news to Tiffany and explain to her why it was so important for people to always reveal crimes against them to authorities immediately instead of keeping secrets. They didn't want her to feel like they were scolding her. Instead, they wanted to assure her they understood why she kept quiet, which was to protect the family, not hide the crime. Tiffany had no choice but to move on with her life, but she would continue counseling as long as her parents felt like she needed it. Now the family would have to move on and pray that Dexter could get past his charges for shooting Paul without having to serve any jail time.

❚ Every moment they spent together was precious, so Levar took a few weeks off from work to spend time with his family. When he returned he was met by the friendly face of Denim Mitchell, who had been God sent since the first time he'd met her. They'd talked off and on over the past few weeks about everything that had happened with Tiffany and Dexter. Now they were ready to get back to work. Denim was a great listener and devoted friend and he would be forever grateful to her for revealing the sordid secret Tiffany was concealing from him and his mother.

While cleaning off all the exercise equipment after closing the clinic, Levar said, "Denim, I want you to come over for dinner one day this week. My mom and Dexter want to thank you for helping Tiffany."

"That's so sweet, Levar, but I haven't talked to Tiffany. Is she mad at me for telling?"

"She seemed relieved that you told so she wouldn't have to."

Denim rolled a large Pilates ball across the room and said, "I don't know."

"It's cool, I promise."

Denim thought about his invitation and then accepted.

"What about tomorrow or is it too short notice?"

He smiled and said, "I think tomorrow will be perfect. I'll let them know."

The next evening, Denim shared a delicious dinner with Levar, Kyra, and the rest of his family. She was a little apprehensive of how Tiffany would receive her, but she was relieved when she gave her a tender hug as soon as she walked through their door. After dinner and for the rest of the evening they were inseparable. Tiffany was excited to show Denim her new room, new iPod, and a few new dance moves as well while they enjoyed two bottles of Pepsi.

"Tiffany, I love your new room and your house."

She laid across her bed and said, "Thanks. Are you going to come to my jump rope competition?"

Denim took a sip of her Pepsi and said, "I wouldn't miss it for the world."

She rolled over onto her back and said, "I wish you were with Levar instead of Kyra."

"I thought you liked Kyra?" Denim asked curiously as she sat in the comfortable chair beside Tiffany's bed.

"She's okay. Levar likes her so I guess that's all that matters. You have a boyfriend anyway."

Denim laughed and then looked at her watch.

"It's getting late. I need to be getting home."

"Already?" Tiffany asked. "It seems like you just got here."

Denim stood and said, "I know, but it is getting late. I'll be back soon."

"You'd better," Tiffany replied as she walked her downstairs to the door. Downstairs, Kyra stood back as Regina, Dexter, Levar, and Tiffany all said their good-byes to Denim. Before walking out the door, Denim waved at Kyra and said, "It was nice seeing you again, Kyra."

Kyra waved back and said, "You too."

While she felt secure in her relationship with Levar, she couldn't help but feel like an outsider and a little jealous of all the attention Denim was getting. She was also a little hurt that Tiffany had confided in Denim instead of her. Levar seemed mesmerized by her charm and now the Banks were under the Denim Mitchell spell. Then just as she was about to go get her jacket and go home, Levar pulled her into his arms and said, "You know I love you, don't you?"

She rubbed her nose against his and said, "Sometimes I wonder, especially when I see how you and your family fall all over Denim."

He put his finger up to her lips to silence her and then said, "I love *you*, Kyra. For the last time, Denim has never been or ever will be a threat to you. Okay?"

Hearing him confess his love for her washed all her jealousy and doubt right out the window. Then for the next hour, they sat on the sofa hand in hand and watched music videos before driving her home.

Denim arrived home just in time to watch the late news with her father. While sitting there she pulled out her diary and made a short entry.

Dear Diary
   Tonight I had a nice dinner with Levar and his family. Tiffany seems happy and I

honestly feel like her nightmare is behind her. One day that monster will get exactly what he deserves. May God have mercy on his soul.
Later,
D

Chapter Thirteen

The moment of truth had come for Dexter as he faced a judge in court to answer to his assault charges. As he sat next to his lawyer, he glanced over at Paul who was sitting with the district attorney presenting the case. Paul was wearing an expensive suit and walking on a cane, which Dexter hoped wouldn't prejudice the jury. Paul had made strides in his recovery but Dexter had hoped he had crippled him enough to put him in a wheelchair for life, but he wasn't so lucky. In any case, he was ready to face his fate and prayed he would get past the charges and be allowed to go home with his family. He looked over his shoulders at Regina and Levar, who were sitting in the courtroom. She blew a kiss at him to give him comfort right before the district attorney approached Dexter's attorney with a plea deal. As the two attorneys whispered back and forth to each other, Regina strained to hear what they were saying but was unsuccessful. Then without any clue to what was going on, the district attorney went back to his table with a piece of paper in hand. Dexter peeked over his shoulder once again and then winked at Regina. Seconds later the bailiff instructed the courtroom to stand and the judge picked up the gavel and called the court to order.

What happened next was short of a miracle. The district attorney stood and announced to the judge that he had met a plea agreement with the defendant and his attorney. Instead of presenting a case of aggravated assault against Dexter, they agreed to a lesser charge of simple or common assault with a suspended sentence. Instead of jail time he would have to attend anger-management classes as part of the agreement. They also worked out a deal to where the charges would be eventually be expunged, leaving his life unblemished. Tears flowed from Regina's eyes as she heard the news. Everyone watched as the judge reviewed the paperwork, signed off on the agreement, slammed the gavel down on his podium, and allowed Dexter to leave court as a free man. Once the case was adjourned everyone stood so the judge could leave. Regina and Levar hugged Dexter as Paul made his way in their direction. Before he could reach them, Dexter noticed him and put his hand up to stop him. He didn't want him to come any closer to him and his family than he already was, so he instructed Levar and Regina to meet him in the hallway and he met Paul halfway. Paul had a smile on his face but Dexter's eyes held the glare of an angry man.

He looked Paul dead in the eyes and said, "Just so there's no misunderstanding, I want you to know that you're dead to me. You should be in jail and one day this will catch up to you. Good-bye."

Dexter walked away without waiting for a response and left the courthouse with his family.

Once home, they were met by Tiffany and their grandparents. Tiffany knew there was a possibility that Dexter might have to go to jail so when she saw him she jumped in his arms and hugged him lovingly. It was a time to rejoice and the family finally felt like they were finally one.

A couple of weeks later, Dexter and Regina took a weeklong honeymoon in Hawaii. While the newlyweds were Hawaii, Paul got back to work as if nothing had ever happened. Then one afternoon after a long day at work he entered the parking garage, climbed into his car, turned on the ignition, and it exploded into a fiery inferno, killing him. Somehow justice had found a way to punish Paul Lindsey. When Dexter and Regina returned from their honeymoon, detectives questioned him about Paul's death but he had an airtight alibi, leaving suspects as the hundreds of lowlife criminals he had unsuccessfully defended and the family members of as many victims. It finally appeared that the family could get back to living.

A few days later they invited all their family and friends over for a large cookout to celebrate the coming together of the two families. Tiffany made amends with Anisa and Laurinda so they could start practicing for a new double Dutch jump rope competition. Levar and Kyra were closer than ever and he was no longer the new intern at the clinic. It was his turn to welcome in a student and show him the ropes. His friendship with Denim had blossomed even more and they'd even started double-dating and sometimes triple-dating with DeMario and Patrice. Life was great and he was so glad he had a loving family who supported him, a girl-friend he loved with all his heart, and a great friend in Denim Mitchell.

Epilogue

Denim was running late to work after forgetting to set her alarm on her clock. She had volunteered to work for another intern so he could go to a concert but had overslept. It was Saturday morning but luckily she had taken a shower and laid out her clothes the night before. As she tied her shoes and grabbed the keys to her car, she hurried out the door to her Mustang. When she climbed in the car she immediately called Dré to leave him a voice message on his cell phone. He was at basketball practice and they had a movie date for later that evening.

After leaving him a sensual message she turned up the volume on her CD player and bobbed her head to the beat of the music. At a traffic light a few blocks from her house she reached up and moved her rearview mirror so she could put on her eyeliner. After applying her eye liner the light turned green and she returned the mirror to its position. That's when she noticed that someone was hiding in her backseat. Fearing for her life, she let out a bloodcurdling scream and nearly hit the car in the lane next to her.

"What are you doing in my car?" she screamed at the top of her lungs.

"Just drive," the voice told her in a whisper. "I have to get as far away from here as I can."